"Stay with me," Giulio whispered, stroking Kate's thigh through the sheet.

"Darling, what are you doing?"

"Tantalizing you.... Think of the pleasures in store for you if we spend the day together."

"It's not that I don't want to," she said, laughing and grabbing his ears, pulling his mouth to hers for a long, satisfying breakfast kiss. The sheet fell from her, and he began kissing her breasts.

"Giulio," she protested, "you'll spill the coffee. Don't you want me to be successful? And sought after by every art director in town?"

"Only from nine to five and never on weekends," he growled, slipping into bed beside her and snuggling her against him . . .

Dear Reader:

Last spring marked SECOND CHANCE AT LOVE's second birthday—and we had good reason to celebrate! While romantic fiction has continued to grow, SECOND CHANCE AT LOVE has remained in the forefront as an innovative, top-selling romance series. In ever-increasing numbers you, the readers, continue to buy SECOND CHANCE AT LOVE, which you've come to know as the "butterfly books."

During the past two years we've received thousands of letters expressing your enthusiasm for SECOND CHANCE AT LOVE. In particular, many of you have asked: "What happens to the hero and heroine after they get married?"

As we attempted to answer that question, our thoughts led naturally to an exciting new concept—a line of romances based on married love. We're now proud to announce the creation of this new line, coming to you next month, called TO HAVE AND TO HOLD.

There has never been a series of romances about marriage. As we did with SECOND CHANCE AT LOVE, we're breaking new ground, setting a new precedent. TO HAVE AND TO HOLD romances will be heartwarming, compelling love stories of marriages that remain exciting, adventurous, sensual and, above all, romantic.

We're very enthusiastic about TO HAVE AND TO HOLD, and we hope you will be too. Watch for its arrival next month. We will, of course, continue to publish six SECOND CHANCE AT LOVE romances every month in addition to our new series. We hope you'll read and enjoy them all!

Warm wishes,

Ellen Edwards

Ellen Edwards
SECOND CHANCE AT LOVE
The Berkley Publishing Group
200 Madison Avenue
New York, N.Y. 10016

A TASTE FOR LOVING
FRANCES DAVIES

**SECOND CHANCE AT LOVE
BOOK**

A TASTE FOR LOVING

To Marilyn,
Carole, and Walter

A TASTE FOR LOVING

CHAPTER ONE

"ONLY THE MOST gifted chefs understand how seductive and sensuous food can be. You're a very clever woman, Miss Elliot."

"I don't cook, Mr. Fraser. I illustrate," said Kate.

Ian Fraser studied her illustration through half-closed eyes. "I can taste the dew on your grapes and the creamy smoothness of your Brie." His tongue flicked over his upper lip, clearly savoring the illusion. "You must be an excellent cook."

"Honestly, I'm not," Kate insisted. "I think I was born with a silver can opener in my hand. But I am an enthusiastic eater."

"Are you really?" He regarded her with renewed interest. "So few women are these days." His voice was almost wistful. "They seem to subsist entirely on seeds and weeds."

"Weeds?"

1

Wiggling all ten fingers toward the ceiling, he mimed a growing plant. "Bales of sprouted legumes garnished with kiwi fruit and dressed with spring water." He shuddered elaborately.

"I have some more illustrations from the cheese book, if you—"

"Didn't you do that cover story on our women's Olympic swim team? Show me something from that," he interrupted.

Kate dug another illustration out of her portfolio and passed it across Fraser's desk.

Tilting his head to one side, he examined it thoughtfully. "Ah hum..." he murmured, smiling.

Kate, who considered herself an authority on the smiles and small animal noises of New York City art directors, smiled brightly back. *Ah hum* usually meant the art director could have used something like this six months ago, but by now the book had gone to press. Of course Ian Fraser was not just any art director. He was one of the superstars, one of the luminaries whom Kate and her designer friends so revered that their names were like the names of saints—filled with light and promise.

And he certainly didn't look at all like the man Kate had envisioned. She had imagined a short, dour, freckled Scot, finicky and withdrawn, while this man who called her work sensuous and seductive was tall and olive skinned, with unruly black hair and sloe-black eyes. Never in a million years would she had expected Ian Fraser to be so—so—

He licked his lips again.

Well, he certainly ought to know sensuous and seductive when he sees it, she thought. She studied him as though she were about to sketch him. That exercise usually kept her calm—but not this time. There was no way, she decided, that any woman could be in the same room with this man and remain calm. She touched her forehead, certain that her temperature had risen several degrees. She sat up straighter, chiding herself for such unprofessional thoughts.

"This is marvelous!" Fraser exclaimed, flinging his arms wide and allowing the illustration to fall to his desk. "It's strong, but sexy." He hunched over the drawing, scrutinizing the details, his powerful hands flat on the desk, fingers splayed.

"That's one of a set of six—I have the printed piece here somewhere," Kate said, once again rooting through her portfolio. How much more would he need to see, she wondered. Her samples were strewn all over his office—on his drawing board, his light table, his desk.

It had been years since an interview with a new art director had made Kate so nervous. She felt more like an auditioning actress than an artist—everything up front: big smile, lots of teeth, and a phony calm covering churning anxiety. Where was that magazine, she asked herself, digging deeper.

Fraser's physical intensity made Kate uneasy. He compelled her attention, and everything in the room seemed to highlight him. He positively radiated passion, fizzed with life. Even his chair was astonishing. It was of caramel-colored oak, so ingeniously carved that the arms and high back seemed to grow out of the roots and tendrils that formed its base. He looks like the Prince of the Dark Forest, Kate mused, sitting on his burnished throne. His eyes were like shaded forest pools...No, he certainly wasn't what she'd thought he'd be.

Kate blinked and shook herself. *Get a hold of yourself,*

girl! You've been illustrating too many children's books. Prince, indeed! She hastily returned her attention to her portfolio.

"You're not at all what I expected, Miss Elliot," remarked the subject of her own very similar thoughts.

Kate pulled her head from the depths of her leather case. "Really?" She smiled blandly.

"From what I'd seen of your work before you walked in here this morning, I'd taken it for granted you'd be very tall and very...hum..."—he tugged at his earlobe, obviously searching for the right word—"very forceful," he concluded lamely, apparently giving up the search.

"Aggressive? Is that the word you're looking for?"

"Yes, I suppose it is."

"It's hardly fair to prejudge someone." Kate flashed what she hoped was a disarming smile.

He chuckled, and his eyes were like laughing water. "No, it's not fair, but it's odd the preconceptions one does form, isn't it? Your work is so strong, so vital, I couldn't believe you were you. I didn't expect a wee redhead not much bigger than her portfolio."

Unable to think of a polite reply, and guiltily aware of her own fantasies, Kate changed the subject. "I'm afraid I don't have that magazine with me, Mr. Fraser. What exactly are you looking for?"

"You're exactly what I'm looking for." He grinned. "May I call you Kate? And please call me Giulio."

"Giulio? Not Ian? I thought—"

"My middle name is Giuliano," he offered with a smile. "My mother's Italian. All my friends call me Giulio." He leaned back in his chair. "Here at Talbot and Beach, as I'm sure you know, we specialize in publishing lavish picture books—on travel, interior design, gourmet cooking, antiques, art—all of which require beautiful photographs and beautiful drawings."

"I have your book on the Royal Ballet; I treasure it."

"That is good, isn't it?" he agreed, beaming. "All those delicious bodies."

Kate was used to art directors talking casually about all aspects of human anatomy, but Fraser savored his words so voluptuously that she wouldn't have been surprised to hear satyr's hooves pawing the carpet beneath his desk.

"What I want to talk to you about is a far cry from the Royal Ballet. Our marketing department, in its infinite wisdom, has decided we should bring out an exercise book for women. I want you to do the drawings."

Kate let out a long, slow breath. She felt as if she'd been holding it for six years. "Drawings? Wouldn't you want to use photographs for a book of that nature?"

"There will be some photos, of course. The author herself is going to be a terrific model for us. She's not a clothes mannequin—all ribs, no hips, and a twelve-inch waist—she's a physiotherapist with an absolutely gorgeous body. Now, I'm convinced that most people find perfect bodies intimidating. Don't you agree?"

He leaned forward, his black eyes traveling so slowly over Kate's seated form, from her earrings to her ankles, that she knew in his mind's eye she sat before him utterly naked. She shivered.

"Don't you agree?" he repeated.

"Oh, yes. I most certainly do," Kate replied with fervor. Throughout her teens she had prayed every night to be tall. By the time she reached twenty and was still five-foot-three, she had found other things to ask for. Now she wondered what Fraser looked like under his silk shirt. "Drawings are easier for people to relate to, I always think," she said, tearing her eyes away from the strong column of his throat.

"Exactly. The author says—and rightly, I'm sure—that if you can visualize the muscles being worked when you exercise, it helps you to feel them. But when you see a photograph of a perfect torso in a leotard, the torso looks lovely but you can't tell what the stomach muscles are doing. And that's where you come in."

"Explain the muscles underneath the leotard."

"Right."

"And how many drawings will you need?"

"Roughly two hundred to two hundred twenty-five."

Whoopee! shouted a small voice in Kate's head. This could buy her her little place in the country. "What will I have to work from?"

"Photographs of the model. You, along with the book's designer, will art direct the shoot. He and the editor have worked out the poses they need, but you'll decide how they should be lighted to show what you'll need for your drawing. What do you think? Does it interest you?"

Kate began furiously multiplying in her head two-hundred-plus drawings times the number of hours probably needed to complete each one. "Mr. Fraser—I'm sorry, Giulio—it's going to take me six to nine months to do that many drawings, depending on how complicated they are." There had to be a catch in this somewhere. No art director could justify to his publisher paying free-lance rates when he had a perfectly good art department right outside his door.

"Yes, Kate, I thought at least nine months. So I'd like you to join Talbot and Beach and work in my art department."

That's the catch, Kate thought. Well, in that case, she'd smile her last smile for Ian Giuliano Fraser. The more she thought about his proposal, the angrier she got. She had wasted two hours exhibiting her work, with nothing to show for it but this idiotic proposal. "Are you asking me to throw over all my accounts to come and work here? I can't do that! That would be completely irresponsible. Besides, I've worked long and hard to get where I am. I'm proud of the work I do, and frankly, I'm appalled that you would suggest such a thing."

"Is your business really all that good?" He seemed genuinely surprised at the vehemence of her refusal. "All the other free-lancers I know tell me business is rotten." His voice grew soft and caressing. "How long have you been working for yourself?" He made it sound as though she were a waif in need of protection.

"Six years. And I like being my own boss. It's as simple as that."

He regarded her thoughtfully. "I doubt that it's really that simple. And I have to admit I didn't expect to be turned down."

One look at him would have been sufficient to convince Kate of the truth of his last statement. Two hours in his presence had more than adequately confirmed for her that Giulio Fraser was not a man who was accustomed to refusals. Well, that's it, Kate thought. Good-bye two-hundred-plus drawings. Good-bye cozy retreat in Woodstock. Damn!

"Look, it's nearly one o'clock," he said. "Why don't we have lunch and talk about this some more afterward?"

"I'm not going to be persuaded by a lunch," Kate warned.

"Perhaps I'll think of something to entice you. Do come," he persisted.

Don't be a fool, a small voice within her said. She knew designers who would kill to get an interview with

Fraser the Great. She should be gracious and go to lunch; it couldn't hurt. Besides, she was dying to know what— or whom—satyrs had for lunch. "Thank you, I'd like to have lunch. May I use your phone first? I should check my answering machine."

"Please," he said, gesturing toward his chair as he rose and left the office.

She gazed after him for a moment, marveling once again at the impressive physique that had come as such a surprise to her. Then, taking her phone beeper from her portfolio, Kate climbed into Fraser's chair. It smelled faintly of lemon oil. She dialed her number, running her fingers over the arms of the chair while she waited for the sound of her own taped voice. The wood felt silky smooth and warm. She cut herself off in mid-sentence by beeping into the phone, and the tape played her messages back to her.

"Kate, this is Angela Rogers at Hill Press. Can you come in tomorrow at three instead of today? Don't call back unless it's a bad time for you. See you then."

"Oh, Kate, I miss you—"

Kate held the receiver away from her ear. "Well, I can't say I've missed you, Neal."

"—be back in town tomorrow. My case has finally gone to the jury, and they shouldn't be out too long. My client's a nervous wreck, but I'm quite confident."

"I'll bet you are." Oh, Neal, I'm sorry, she thought, but you do get on my nerves. He was a pleasant enough companion for a movie or an occasional dinner, but his endless talk of torts and writs bored her beyond words, and his blind insistence that they were meant for each other had curdled her friendly affection for him.

"I'll call you when I get in."

"Hi, Kate. It's Betty at Typesetting, Inc. I know we

promised you proofs by five o'clock, but the computer's down again. We're working on it."

After Betty there was silence on the tape. Kate hung up.

Perched in Fraser's chair, her feet dangling inches above the floor, she surveyed his office. This had been an interesting experience, anyway, she consoled herself. She tried to commit every detail to memory, knowing that there weren't that many designer's who ever got past Fraser's door. There were the expected long tables and enormous flat files. A wall of books reached to the ceiling. Every available surface was stacked with covers, printed proofs, roughs; her own work was there now, too, of course. It was a friendly, creative chaos she readily understood.

She swiveled the chair to look at the large chart she had glimpsed behind his back. It was the room's only wall hanging: a large, elaborately detailed manuscript flow chart, its colored patterns mapping the course of all the books in progress at Talbot and Beach. Titles were listed at the left edge, production deadlines down the center, and publication dates at the extreme right. Reading down the left-hand side, Kate was startled to find, *BODY BOOK, by Gunilla Gunderson. Editor: Elizabeth Madden; designer: Jeffrey Stewart; illustrator: Kate Elliot.*

"Well, well, well! You're pretty sure of yourself, aren't you Mr. Fraser?" she murmured to herself. Was he really that certain she'd join his department, or was he, perhaps, prepared for a little old-fashioned hard bargaining before he hired her as a free-lancer after all? Was he just playing games? Well, it would take two to play— and she was ready!

What would it be like to sit in this chair someday as

art director—to have platoons of designers and photographers and illustrators poised to carry out her ideas, she wondered. The first thing she'd add would be a footstool, she decided with a giggle. Her reverie was interrupted by a knock on the door.

"Come in," she called imperiously in her new art director's voice. Then she blushed in embarrassment and scrambled out of the giant chair just as Fraser strode in with his arm around a chubby koala bear.

Kate guessed the cheerful man was a good ten years older than Fraser—somewhere on the other side of fifty. The top of his shiny pink head barely reached Fraser's shoulder. Straw-colored fur sprang in a fringe around his bald spot, and his eyebrows were so thick she couldn't see his bright button eyes until he raised his chin. One of the denizens of the prince's forest, she decided.

"Kate, this is Jeffrey Stewart. Jeff, Kate Elliot. Jeffrey's going to design the book, Kate. I thought you two might like to talk."

The koala bear took Kate's hand in two chubby paws. "I'm delighted to meet you. I admire your work, and I'm looking forward to our collaboration."

"Thank you, but I haven't yet agreed to do the book."

"You haven't?" Two furry brows waggled upward in surprise.

"It doesn't hurt to talk," Fraser broke in, his black eyes twinkling at her. "Take Kate around the corner," he directed Jeffrey. "I'll collect Liz and meet you there."

CHAPTER TWO

CINNAMON. THE SCENT of cinnamon was the first thing Kate noticed as they stepped through the restaurant door. Then so many mingled spices overwhelmed her that she couldn't identify a single one. A cascade of sitar music sprinkled her with silver droplets of sound.

The turbaned maître d' towered above them. "Mr. Fraser's table?" he murmured to Jeffrey.

"Yes, thank you, Mr. Mohan. We'll be four today."

"Right this way, please."

The moment they were seated, Jeffrey turned to Kate and answered her question even before she could ask it. "What's Giulio like to work for? Marvelous, maddening, exhilarating, and utterly exhausting."

"I can believe that," she said.

"You'd learn a lot working for him; everyone does who's willing to learn. He's a perfectionist and absolutely relentless in the pursuit of what he wants. If you're a

11

sensitive flower, he'll walk all over you. If you're as tough as he is, you'll be fine."

"I'd begun to suspect that," she said thoughtfully.

"I hope you'll decide to do the book; I know I'd enjoy working with you."

"Thank you. Fraser and I may be able to come to an agreement." He did have her name on his chart, after all. Well, why not? She would try to work out something, if the terms were acceptable. A commission from Fraser would be a terrific boost for her career.

She looked up to see the man in question walking toward them. How vivid he looked next to the pale, elegant woman on his arm. She wore a white linen suit piped in palest blue; ash blond hair cascaded to her shoulders. She was so thin she appeared fragile as she placed each foot carefully in front of the other with the delicacy of a water bird. Another of the prince's forest creatures, Kate reflected.

"Liz," Fraser said, "let me introduce Katherine Elliot. Kate, this is Elizabeth Madden. Liz is the editor of the *Body Book*. We keep calling it that for lack of something better. I don't know when they're going to settle on a title."

"How do you do, Miss Madden," Kate said, rising and offering her hand. Miss Madden extended her wrist, and her hand and fingers flowed after. She laid three cool fingertips briefly against Kate's warm palm and as quickly withdrew them.

"Do call me Liz," she said, her gray eyes opening wide as she took a seat and focused on Kate. "Giulio tells me you drew that seven-layer sandwich for the New Country Bread campaign—the one I saw on all the buses last fall. It shot my diet all to hell."

"I'm sorry," Kate said, simultaneously wondering how

anyone that thin could need to diet. Liz could have slipped through the eye of a needle while carrying her handbag.

"I stood it for three weeks, then I went out and bought a loaf and built the most glorious sandwich that ever was—I even put in anchovies, and I'm not that crazy about anchovies—and I sat down and ate it for my dinner. It was wonderful!" Her eyes glazed in memory. "Then I fasted for four days, didn't I, darling?" She turned to Fraser for confirmation.

"Liz collects diets," Fraser elaborated, "the way other people collect limited editions or oyster plates." He slipped an arm around Liz, hugging her in a gesture of such easy intimacy that Kate could feel the special bond between them. It made her strangely wistful.

Liz laughed good-naturedly. "The worst one was that awful Norwegian one—"

"The Namsos Diet," Fraser finished for her.

"All fish and that weird brown cheese that tastes like Fels Naptha."

"*Gjetost?*" Kate guessed.

"That's the one," Liz affirmed grimly.

"I seem to remember," said Jeffrey, "that at the time, Giulio said the Great Beet Diet was the worst."

"It was," Fraser agreed. "And still is. Boiled beets, beet salads, beet soups—Liz grew pinker and pinker—shredded beets, beet frappés . . . After a month her bellybutton looked like a raspberry."

"I knew I was in trouble when I took off my nail polish and my nails were still red. Today's a salad day, darling. So just the marinated cucumbers for me, and perhaps some mint tea."

"I hope you like Indian food," Fraser said to Kate.

"I don't really know it at all," she said. Nothing she had seen the waiters carrying looked or smelled anything like her friend Marion's Wednesday night curry of Sunday's leftover chicken. The moment she opened the menu she knew she was lost. The curries filled an entire page, followed by pages of dishes she'd never even heard of. Kormas? Birianis? Pilaus must be pilafs, she decided, and kebabs she knew, but what was nan? There were exotic vegetable dishes and six different kinds of dal. Dal? There was even a dal of the day!

"Shall I order for you?" Fraser asked, gazing directly into her eyes.

"Yes, please," she said, vastly relieved.

While he ordered, Kate turned to Jeffrey, who had been describing his weekend to Liz.

"And then on Sunday," he said, "I went to the most marvelous concert. Thirty-two mandolins at Carnegie Recital Hall."

Kate laughed, and Liz looked pained.

"Hey, come on," he said. "This was serious." He drew himself up in mock hauteur. "They played Mozart and Telemann and Kabalevsky and—"

Now Fraser was laughing, too. "Have you found any new roller coasters for this summer, Jeffrey?" He turned his gleaming dark gaze to Kate. "You should be warned now, Kate, that this designer of the world's most fastidiously elegant books has one consuming passion: the pursuit of the world's most terrifying roller coasters."

Kate tried very hard to imagine koala-bear Jeffrey riding a roller coaster, but she couldn't manage it. The best she could do was Paddington Bear waving from the top of a Ferris wheel.

"There's a new one near Chicago," Jeffrey enthused. "It makes three complete loops. I'm going to go out there for a weekend next month." His button eyes glittered with anticipation. "And how was your weekend, Liz?

Did you and Giulio go up to Len Cutter's place?"

"I found it very restful," Liz responded. "Marie and I lazed on the deck for two days playing Scrabble while Len and Giulio went off and did manly things in the woods. Each time they came in, they were bursting with goatish virility and reeking of sweat, and all because they'd chopped a few sticks of firewood."

"We did more than that," Fraser protested. "We put in two dozen rosebushes and a shadblow tree."

Kate found herself listening to the teasing argument with a mixture of curiosity and dismay. But her attention was soon diverted.

A flurry of waiters appeared with covered dishes, and when the silver lids were whisked away the table was laden with a paradise of color. A gleaming brass platter sizzled with scarlet pieces of chicken, silvery onion slices, and shiny yellow wedges of lemon. There were bright green beans, tiny brown meatballs in a golden sauce, and a peaked snowdrift of rice flecked with pimentoes, peas, and toasted nuts. A dark orange puree filled a deep bowl, and a woven basket lined with a red cloth brimmed with puffed rounds of bread. Chutneys, glowing on a silver tray, ranged from deepest mahogany through red to mint-green and snowy coconut.

Kate shook her head in wonder. It was not in her nature to pretend to a sophistication she didn't have. "It's beautiful," she uttered.

Fraser smiled broadly at her and winked. "For the eyes of hungry artists." He then served a little from each dish onto her plate, lovingly explaining each one. The puré was the dal, made from a variety of split peas and spices. The beans had been blanched; the rice—Kate gave up trying to remember it all and sampled the chicken. It was crisp and pungent on the outside, meltingly tender inside. The beans were delicate and fragrant with ginger.

"You must dip your bread—it's called parotha—in the dal," Giulio advised. "Go ahead, scoop it up."

The bread was a buttery cloud of gossamer layers. She dipped a piece into the dal and tasted. A subtle rainbow of flavors burst in her mouth—the prickly browns of cinnamon and clove, dark cumin, and bright coriander. The other spices were so intertwined that their flavors mingled and they remained a mystery to her. She mixed a dollop of the beautiful green chutney in her next scoop. As she took a bite, tears welled in her eyes.

"Oh! That's not just mint—that's *hot!*" she cried, reaching for her glass of cold beer. "What is that?" she asked when she caught her breath.

"Mint and green chili peppers," Giulio said. "Do you like it?" he asked solicitously.

"It's wonderful!" she said, tears streaming down her cheeks.

Jeffrey laughed. "Giulio, I think you've made another convert."

"I'd like some more tea, darling," Liz interjected calmly.

Giulio ordered Liz's tea and heaped Kate's plate again. She happily ate her way through it.

"Beware of the desserts, Kate," Liz warned. "They all taste like cheap perfume."

"I've eaten so much I couldn't manage one anyway," Kate replied. "I'd have to dab it behind my ears."

It was only when Kate was seated once more in his office that she realized she had begun thinking of him as Giulio rather than Fraser. She was no longer so wary of the man. She warned herself to be careful. She was letting him soften her up.

"I'd like you to give serious consideration to my proposition," he said, his voice soft and coaxing. "Come work for me."

"I've told you, I can't."

"I'd really like to have you right here—to work on this book. Think how much easier it would be for you if you had access to—our facilities." He was staring at her mouth.

"That's really not essential." Involuntarily she licked her lips.

He leaned forward. "I like some of the product photography you've directed. I have another project . . ." His voice grew softer and softer, and Kate had to strain toward him to catch his last words.

If he kept this up, he'd hypnotize her, she suddenly realized, deciding there should be a law against anyone having eyes that big and black. Why did he keep looking at her mouth? Kate sat up with a start—she had completely lost track of what he was saying.

". . . so you see, I think we could work quite well together. Do come work for me."

She took a deep breath. "I can't. I thought I'd made myself clear before we went to lunch. If I dumped the clients I have now, where would I be when I finished your job? I'd be starting all over. I don't think you understand. My loyalty to my clients aside, I truly value my independence."

"Are you sure the independence you prize so highly isn't an excuse for not taking on greater responsibilities?"

"Of course I'm sure."

"Haven't you carved out a snug little niche for yourself where you don't have to meet any new challenges? How long did you say you'd been free-lancing? Six years? You must be twenty-eight. It's time you began taking on real challenges."

The gaze he fixed on her alerted her senses to a challenge other than the artistic one under discussion, and she struggled to bring her thoughts back to a professional plane. "Mr. Fraser, the work I'm doing *is* challenging. It's diversified, and yes, my niche is snug. I've made it that way through my own efforts, and I enjoy the comfort, thank you very much. And I'm twenty-nine, by the way."

He leaned back in his chair, his arms folded across his chest, his face an unreadable mask. But his eyes had returned to her mouth.

If he wasn't going to budge from his position, neither was she. "I'd better pack my things," Kate said at last.

He stood up. "You're obstinate, Elliot. You're stubborn, but you're also talented. Maybe we can work out a compromise."

Kate said nothing, waiting patiently. Let him show his cards, she decided, so she could determine whether he was offering a compromise or a finesse.

"Let's say we pay you a lump sum—less, admittedly, than your free-lance rate—but with a royalty on each book that could more than make up the difference."

"Plus a credit line on the title page," she added.

"Now wait a minute—"

"And another on the dust jacket, in at least twenty-four point type," she shot back.

"Aren't you getting carried away?" He was obviously warming to the battle.

"No," she said emphatically, "I am not."

"Twenty-four point is ridiculously large. Sixteen or nothing."

"Twenty!"

"Eighteen!"

"Agreed!" she said with relish.

"However," he said, watching her closely, "you must have the work completed within nine months."

"Nine months?"

"Without fail. How you fit your other work in is your problem. What do you say? Will you think about it and call me tomorrow? Meanwhile I'll talk to the money boys and see if they'll part with a royalty for you."

So, the royalty was his trump card, Kate thought. Was there a way she could meet his deadline and do her other work, too? If she was stubborn, he was relentless, just as Jeffrey had said. What if she agreed to do the drawings for less and the book didn't sell? But then, what if it sold like crazy? What if—

"What do you say?" he repeated.

"I'll think about it."

Suddenly he was all smiles. "Splendid! Now let me help you pack that monster portfolio."

Kate stood at the curb, hailing a cab and attempting to reconcile in her own mind the gentle, considerate man who had given her lunch with the determined, single-minded bargainer who wanted her to throw over everything she'd worked to achieve. He really was the most infuriating man she'd ever met, she thought, as she wrenched open the taxi door, heaved her portfolio inside, and sank, all too quickly, into the springless backseat.

"Fifty-sixth Street," she said, "between Eighth and Ninth."

"Hey," the driver said, catching her eye in his rear-view mirror. "How does a little lady like you lug that big case around all day?"

"It's easy," she lied.

"Jeeze."

That didn't seem to require an answer, so she made none.

"Me, I'm just driving this week to help out my brother-in-law. He was nosing into the left lane over on Park when this other cab cuts him off. So he gets mad. I mean, who wouldn't, y'know? Anyway, they're both caught by the light—my brother-in-law in the right lane, this jerk in the left. So my brother-in-law, he, uh—makes this gesture at the other cabbie, but good, y'know?"

"I can imagine it, yes."

"Then all of a sudden this fantastic broad gets out of the back of the other cab. I mean fantastic—must be six-foot in heels—she's wearing a suit and this fur thing around her neck, the whole bit—so, quick as a flash she's out of the other cab and grabs my brother-in-law's finger where it's still pointing up, and she gives it this bone-crushing twist. Then she whips back into the cab and they're gone. Jeeze. All gorgeousness on the outside, and inside she's like iron. Now ain't that incredible?"

"Not really. I think I just had lunch with her twin brother."

Slowly, with voluptuous pleasure, Kate eased off her shoes. Heaven, she thought and sighed. Pure heaven. She had just put the kettle on for tea when Marion called. Marion, too, had traveled far since Kate's first years in New York, when Kate and Marion and Peggy had shared a tiny apartment and pooled their slender earnings. Peggy had married a television producer, and Marion worked as executive assistant to the director of a charitable trust.

"Where have you been?" Marion demanded. "I've been calling you all day. What happened with Fraser? What did he want? What's the great man like?"

"He's the most obstinate, stubborn, iron-willed man I've ever met. Can you believe he had put my name down on his publication chart before he even met me? How's that for gall?"

"He must really want you. But what for?"

"Two hundred or so drawings."

"Wow! Well, what happened? What did he say?"

"First he tried to talk me into coming to work for him, but I absolutely refused."

"Good for you . . . I guess."

"Besides, I'm sure I could never work really closely with that man. He may be one of the greatest designers of our time and all that, but—there's something about him—I'm not sure what it is, but—"

"Do I detect a hint of animal interest there?"

"No!"

"What does he look like?"

"The Prince of the Dark Forest."

"Oh, boy! Tell me more."

"There's something disturbing—and terribly commanding—about that man. He's physically compelling. Without lifting a finger he makes you aware of this terrific strength of will."

"He sounds pretty sexy to me."

"Well, to be honest, he is—but I'm not all that ready to be compelled."

"So you turned him down flat?"

"Not exactly. He finally suggested a compromise, which I agreed to consider."

"You can't have spent the whole day arguing."

"No, he bought me—along with the book's designer, Jeffrey Stewart, and Elizabeth Madden, the editor—a spectacular Indian lunch. Stewart's a darling man; he looks like a bear in a children's book. But Madden is right out of a book for grown-ups. *Très, très soignée:* wraith thin, a thirty-two-Chicklet smile—"

"I think I hate her. What was she wearing?"

"An exquisite white linen suit—a Millie Juste, I think—with the palest blue piping and just the tiniest thread of a horizontal blue stripe. Now that I think of it, she looked rather like an index card—if she turned sideways you'd see only an edge. I gather she and Fraser are a thing."

"What a shame."

"And I'm sure I scandalized her by eating everything in sight."

"Tell me more about Fraser."

"Well, my mother would have called him an attractive brute. My grandmother would have called him a rake."

"And what would you call him?"

"A stubborn, iron-willed—"

"You said all that—"

"Voluptuary." A thin, nerve-shredding whistle shrieked from the kitchen. "Kettle's boiling. I'll call you tomorrow and tell you what I decide."

When Kate went to bed that night, she still hadn't decided what to do. She lay staring at the ceiling and debating with herself. What Giulio was offering wasn't a bad compromise, but how could she work comfortably with a man who never stopped undressing her with his eyes? On the other hand, she wasn't being paid to feel comfortable. She punched her pillow and turned on her side. Jeffrey was the book's designer, after all, so she probably wouldn't see that much of Giulio anyway. Why had he kept staring at her mouth? She'd report directly to Jeffrey, she reminded herself. She flopped onto her stomach. It would be marvelous to be able to buy her little farmhouse. And it would be an enormous challenge, doing the book . . . and if challenge made the man, what made the woman? It wasn't as if she couldn't handle Giulio if she ran into him at the office. She was almost tempted to take the job just to prove to him she could do it in *less* than nine months. Just to see the look on his face. How could anyone have eyes so black . . . ?

CHAPTER THREE

BIRDS SANG IN the tree tops high above her where the topmost branches caught the sun's last light. Small animals scurried away unseen in the underbrush. It grew colder. Soon it would be dark. Kate turned in a circle, but she could see no path through the enclosing bracken. Her arms and legs stung with scratches; burrs clung to her skirt. She was tired and frightened. Suddenly she heard Neal calling to her; she couldn't see him, but she heard him quite clearly.

"Halloo," he called. "Halloo. I'm late for court, late for court."

"Where are you?" she shouted after his echoing voice, but there was no reply.

A beautiful white bird landed at her feet, cocked its graceful head at her, and said, "Don't eat the berries, dear. They taste like cheap perfume."

Then there was a great crashing in the forest, and

Fraser strode up to her. He had vine leaves in his hair, and he looked like Bacchus, the god of wine. He carried an enormous bunch of purple grapes high over his head as though in celebration of some ancient rite or revel.

"Are you hungry? I've brought you something to eat." His voice was seductive, and his eyes were aflame. He slipped a purple grape between her lips, and a succulent sweetness unlike anything she had ever tasted filled her mouth with an intoxicating liquor.

"Oh!" she cried in surprise and delight. Then his lips took hers, his tongue searching hungrily for the lingering sweetness.

Kate awoke shaking, her nightgown drenched. "How could I dream something like that?" she muttered, half in anger, half in wonder "How *could* I?" She threw off her blanket, marched herself smartly into her tiny kitchen, and put on a pot of coffee.

Examining her reflection in the bathroom mirror, she pronounced it seedy. Decidedly seedy. "You cannot," she said, shaking her toothbrush at the woman in the mirror, "subdue the monster you fear unless you're willing to face it. So shape up!" She was vigorously alternating brushing and spitting when the phone rang.

"Murf?" she said, swallowing a minty mouthful.

"Good morning. This is Giulio Fraser. Did I wake you?"

"Certainly not," she said indignantly. Unless you deliberately invaded my dreams, she added silently.

"I've just talked to the boys who hold the purse strings, and they've agreed to give you a couple of royalty points. What do you say? Will you do it?"

Kate took a deep breath. "I say yes, Giulio Fraser. Yes."

"Splendid! Be here next Wednesday morning at nine for a meeting with Liz and Jeffrey," he ordered. "Liz's office. If I'm not here, she'll have your contract. You'll be shooting the model at midnight Wednesday—Liz will explain all that—so leave Thursday open. Have you had your breakfast?"

"No, not yet," she admitted reluctantly. "I don't usually have more than coffee and toast anyway."

"Eat fruit," he commanded.

"What?"

"I said, eat some fruit. It's good for you." He hung up.

What kind of monster is he, she mused, going around telling maidens to eat fruit? Then she remembered the purple grapes and, blushing so hard that even the soles of her feet were burning, she forced herself to take a bone-chilling shower.

As she did every weekday morning, Kate spent an hour on the telephone. Curled up in one corner of her couch, her feet tucked under her, her second cup of coffee at her elbow and her schedule diary open on her lap, she answered her taped messages, called accounts, built fires under slow typesetters, pleaded with sluggish color labs. Now she listened with a skepticism based on long experience to a printer's sorrowful lament about spoilage.

Finishing her calls, she briefly reflected on how much she enjoyed her solitude, working alone, comfortably inhabiting a world of her own devising, free from the daily demands her former life-style had made on her. She cherished both the repetition and the variety of the daily tasks that gave shape to her life. Messengers brought her packages from suppliers and clients. Other messengers carried away her finished work.

Unwinding herself from the sofa, she moved to perch at her drawing board next to the windows, high above the street below. She scanned the northern skies and felt like an island lighthouse keeper as thunderheads scudded in from the west. She was a secret observer of life in the building opposite. Old and venerable, it wore its ancient coat of grime with the dignity of a grandmother wrapped in a comforting shawl.

At noon she looked across to "the Actress's" window. Yes, she was up. Her ginger cat sat in the window, smiling his evil smile at a pigeon huddled on the sill.

Window washing was the first job Kate had tackled on the day she'd moved into her apartment on Manhattan's West Side, near both the theater district and the bustling midtown office area. She had stood on her inside sill, scrubbing away and wondering if the building owners ever washed the outside, when she saw a woman in the apartment opposite open her kitchen window to strew crumbs on the sill. My word, she'd said to herself. That's—that's—um... She knew she was a famous actress, but she couldn't think of her name. She'd stood there, feeling like a ninny, plastered against the glass, staring, trying desperately to think of her name, when the Actress had looked up and seen her. She'd smiled her famous smile, and Kate had smiled weakly back, embarrassed to be caught staring. Rosalind Cousins! That's Rosalind Cousins, she had remembered at last. But even after four years, she still thought of her as the Actress.

At twelve-thirty precisely, the Actress opened her window to strew her handful of crumbs. She looked over, as always, and spotted Kate at her drawing board. Kate smiled and waved, and the Actress, as always, smiled and waved back.

At two-thirty Kate packed up her dust-jacket layouts for Hill Press. They were a good account—Kate had been working for them steadily for six years.

"Did you like the book?" asked Angela Rogers, Hill Press's art director.

Kate prided herself on never having done a cover for a book she had not read. "I liked it very much," she said.

It was the story of a young woman who fled both her husband and her lover to hide away in Amsterdam until she sorted out her life. Kate had found it a heart rending story of loneliness and despair. She had wept over the galleys at the end.

"I've brought you a slide," Kate announced. "Put this in your projector."

The picture showed a stone terrace in the spring. Metal tables and chairs had been put out, but their positions were askew, as if the occupants had left hastily, driven indoors by a sudden shower. A film of water on the terrace reflected the abandoned furniture. The trees beyond were a haze of green, just coming into leaf and bud. They gave promise of life to come, but the sky was dark with rain, the air filled with mists. The life promised seemed far away, the picture filled with loneliness and despair.

"This is perfect," said Angela. "Wherever did you get it? Where is it?"

"It's the terrace of the Stedelijk Museum in Amsterdam. I took it myself, actually . . . some years ago . . . on my honeymoon."

"Why, Kate, I never knew you were married."

"It was mercifully brief." For a moment she remembered Amsterdam—and the honeymoon that was a promise unfulfilled. She shook herself and turned to Angela, all business.

"The title can go up in the sky—here, as I've shown on the rough. I can send this out for separations as soon as you get approval from your marketing people. I'll need the rest of the jacket copy. Do you have an author photo?"

"Yes, everything's here," Angela confirmed, handing over a manila envelope.

"I'll have reader proofs for you in a couple of days."

"So you were married... aren't you the sly one, though?" Angela regarded her quizzically for a long time. When she finally broke the silence, her tone was conspiratorial. "May I tell you something in confidence?"

"Of course, but are you sure you want to?"

"I'm leaving Hill Press in eight months—next December."

"Where are you going? To which publisher?"

"I'm not going to another publisher. I'm getting married, Kate. I'm quitting." Her eyes shone, and her face was flushed.

"That's wonderful, Angela. I'm very happy for you. But why are you quitting?"

"To be perfectly honest, I feel like I'm being rescued. It's going to be wonderful to depend on someone else again. Richard doesn't mind my working, but I think marriage has to be a full-time job. I'm convinced that's why both my marriages failed. I wasn't a full-time wife, and I should have been. This time around I'm going to make a real home for my husband. You've been married—don't you agree that's the only way?"

"It wasn't for me. It wasn't enough."

"Well, it's going to be enough for this girl, I can tell

you. I don't know about you, but I never expected to work for the rest of my life." She smiled dreamily at her sparkling engagement ring. "The rest of my life belongs to Richard."

Oh, Angela, Kate thought, you're making a mistake. Kate was shocked. What fears had reduced this successful, coolly self-sufficient woman to simpering jelly? Kate's heart ached for her, and she tried to banish her skepticism. Perhaps Angela's arrangement would work for her, even if it hadn't for Kate.

"No one here knows yet that I'm leaving, except the publisher and the editorial director. In a couple of months we'll begin interviews for a new art director. I'd like to recommend you for the job. Would you be interested?"

"Me? That's crazy, Angela. I've never been an art director."

"You have to start sometime. You really can't go on free-lancing forever."

"Why not?"

Angela ignored the question. "Aside from procedural things, there's really nothing about my job you don't already know how to do. You don't have to give me an answer this week or even this month, but promise me you'll think about it. I'd like to put your name at the top of my candidates list."

Angela was the second person in two days to try convincing her to give up free-lancing. This was different from Giulio's offer, though. She wouldn't be just another member of a huge department—she'd be art director herself. Hill Press was a very small company with a small design staff, but still . . . No, she told herself, Angela was loopy. This wouldn't be right for Kate Elliott. She wasn't like Angela; she didn't want to be tied down. And she certainly hadn't spent a whole day arguing the same issue with Giulio Fraser only to succumb to Angela.

"It's very generous of you to offer," she said. "And I will think about it." Time enough later to tell Angela she wouldn't do it. Angela's romance had obviously clouded her judgment in more ways than one.

CHAPTER FOUR

JEFFREY STEWART WAS already in Liz Madden's office when Kate arrived for her appointment the following week.

"Did Giulio tell you about our marathon photo session?" he asked. "It starts at midnight tonight at the Uptown Health Club. That way we'll have twelve hours to shoot. We can have the gym to ourselves until noon."

"Won't your model be wiped out after a couple of hours?" Kate asked.

Liz laughed. "Not our Gunilla. Wait till you meet her."

"Who's the photographer?" Kate queried.

"Melissa Edwards," said Jeffrey.

"But she's one of the biggest names in fashion," Kate protested. "Isn't that overkill, just to take pictures for me to work from?"

"There'll be some photos in the book, you know," Liz pointed out. "And of course we need a cover shot. And luckily for us, Melissa's an old friend of Giulio's *and* she had a hole in her schedule. I think we should talk about what Gunilla should wear. Kate, what do you suggest?" She handed Kate some prints from a stack of Polaroids.

"They're not very helpful, I'm afraid," Jeffrey said apologetically.

The pictures showed a beautifully proportioned woman dressed, like a dancer, in black tights and a long-sleeved black leotard. The costume revealed nothing but Gunilla's trim silhouette.

"You're right," Kate agreed. "This won't do at all. I'd like to see as much musculature as possible. How about a string bikini?"

"No good," Liz vetoed. "Floor burns or mat burns or whatever."

"Oh. Well . . ." Kate began. They both stared at her, obviously waiting for her suggestion. "Why not a flesh-colored tank-top leotard and tights, and we'll spray the fabric down with glycerin and water so that it really clings. The heat of the floodlights will keep her warm."

Liz and Jeffrey nodded their approval. The three of them spent the next several hours going over Liz's log of poses required. Jeffrey discussed which ones would be treated as major drawings, which as minor ones or details.

It was noon when Kate left the building. Office workers streamed through the lobby toward the soft May sunshine. Caught up in the crowd, Kate was crushed in the doorway until the press of those behind her popped her through like a cork, smack into a man's arms.

"I'm so sorry," she said, her mouth muffled against his shirt.

"I'm not," came the murmured response. Giulio didn't release her. Instead, he stood smiling down at her, his arms tightly enclosing her, sheltering her from the rushing throng. "Come have lunch with me, little Elliot." His voice was warm, and his eyes looked deeply into hers.

The crowd around them vanished utterly. Gone was the babble of voices and the hum of traffic. Kate could hear only his voice, feel only his arms, and a tingling like an electrical charge raced up and down her spine. This was crazy, she told herself.

"Have you eaten?" he asked.

"No, I, uh—"

"Come with me." He tucked her arm firmly beneath his and strode off down the street with Kate trotting beside him to keep up.

The restaurant was small and crowded. The long counter on their right was completely filled by dark-suited Japanese businessmen who were eating bite-sized portions of garnished rice as quickly as the three countermen could assemble the morsels.

Giulio introduced her to the proprietor, who found them a quiet table in the back.

"Do you have a favorite sushi?" Giulio said. "Or sashimi?"

"Why don't you order for both of us," suggested Kate, who had never tasted either.

The waiter placed a bamboo tray of steaming hot towels between them.

"Have you always been interested in ethnic restaurants?" she asked, gratefully wiping her hands.

"It runs in my family. My mother's a marvelous cook—

she taught me to cook, as a matter of fact—and discovering new restaurants has always been a kind of family hobby. The most exciting discoveries are always the little family-run places, like this one or Mohan's, where the dishes served are the family's heritage, prepared without compromises and served with real pride." His eyes were alight with enthusiasm. "Where do you think is the best and least pretentious place to sample regional American specialties?"

"I give up. Where?"

"A church social!" he said in a voice hushed with reverence. "Have you ever been to a Greek Orthodox church picnic where they roast whole lambs on spits?"

She shook her head. She had never heard of anyone in Minneapolis spitting lambs.

"I know a Baptist church," he whispered so softly he might have been divulging a state secret, "where, on the first Sunday in August, the preacher's wife makes the finest Southern-fried chicken on this earth."

"If you don't stop, I may start eating this towel," Kate protested.

"Are you a good cook?" he demanded abruptly.

"I thought I'd explained all that. I hardly cook at all, I'm afraid—just enough to keep from starving. I think of it as cooking in self-defense." Kate was surprised at how apologetic she sounded. Why was she trying to justify herself to this man, she wondered. It wasn't a sin to open cans. Not everyone could be a Julia Child.

Mercifully the waiter chose that moment to set before them the most artfully arranged, exquisite-looking food Kate had ever seen.

"Explain, please," Kate directed. And Giulio did.

Little pillows of rice were arranged on a red lacquer tray. The grains of rice shone with the luster and translucence of seed pearls. Some of the pillows were topped with bits of vegetables, others with thin slices of fish. In some the rice had been rolled around matchstick thin slices of cucumber or scallion and wrapped in a green vegetable leaf and sliced. Still others were rolled in a thin omelet. Flowers were formed from shavings of pink ginger. Tiny mountains of grated radish rose from sea-blue dishes. Diminutive white lotus-petal dishes held pale green horseradish and dark pools of pungent dipping sauce.

Kate leaned across the table. "Do I have to pick them up with these chopsticks? I'll never manage it."

"No. Look at the men up at the counter. Most of them use their fingers."

"Why is the fish topping cold?" she asked.

"Well, hum . . . the rice is cold, after all, so there's no point in serving it hot, is there?"

"No, I suppose not. It's delicious. The flavor's so delicate." She tried another one. "It makes me think of sea air and sparkling waves and brilliant anemones."

Giulio laughed and surveyed her with undisguised delight. "You may not be a born cook, but I think you're a born eater." His smile subsided slightly, and he asked, "Did Liz have the contract for you to sign?"

She nodded, her mouth full of tangy rice.

"I'm sorry you didn't accept my first offer," he said quietly. "It would be—interesting to have you in the office next to mine every day. Think of the lunches we could have," he went on so suggestively that she couldn't believe he was just talking about meals.

"It never rains, but it pours."

"What do you mean?"

"I can't say who it is, but someone else just last week

tried to talk me into giving up free-lance work—this time to become an art director."

"A publishing house?"

"Yes."

"Good. Do it." He leaned toward her, looking earnest now, not bullying as he had been during their first meeting. "You're caught in a trap, Kate. It's not your fault, but it's one many talented free-lancers get caught in. You need something—or someone—to give you a boost out of it."

"I don't feel trapped."

"That's the insidious part of it. The biggest job you'll get in a year will be something like mine—or maybe the annual report for Megabucks, Limited."

"That's not peanuts."

"I know, but will Megabucks call you when they want to overhaul their corporate image? No. They'll call Chermayeff. And why did they come to you for their annual report? Because the third vice-president saw what you did for the Porridge Council of America, had the good sense to like it, and now he wants exactly the same thing for Megabucks. Am I right?"

"Yes," she admitted reluctantly. "You're right."

"Kate, a career doesn't just happen; you don't slide into it like a warm bath. You must plan it, nurture it. You've done fairly well for yourself so far; now you've got to prove you can take on bigger things, new things— prove that you can handle problems with depth and scope. Time put into demonstrating that to the marketplace is an investment in your future. If you put in five years or so as an art director with a really good house, you can return to free-lancing with a client list beyond your wildest dreams today."

"I'd never thought of it like that."

"It's time you did."

The entire platter was empty. "Would you like some more?" he asked.

"I don't think I could possibly—"

"Suppose I order just six—three each."

"Then could we have some with that lovely dark fish on top? What is that, by the way?"

"That's tuna. It doesn't taste like that smelly stuff from cans, does it?" he asserted, smiling.

When the second, much smaller, tray of sushi arrived, Giulio prompted, "Did your meeting with Jeffrey and Liz go all right? Any problems?"

"No, it was fine."

"I expect your drawings to be strong—that's your style—but you mustn't be afraid of a little overemphasis. I want to see a woman exulting in her womanhood, in physical well-being, in health. Some sensuousness will be perfectly fine. After all, a healthy woman *is* sexy. Nipples are out, but bellybuttons are okay."

"Really?" Kate laughed, once again slightly flustered by the graphic references she was usually so comfortable with. "Are you going to eat that last piece?" she asked, steering the conversation away from nipples and navels.

"No, go ahead." He leaned back in his chair, smiling broadly. "I can't tell you what a joy it is to share a meal with a woman who really enjoys eating." He regarded her through half-closed eyes.

Again she watched his eyes travel down over her torso and back up to her mouth. Kate caught her breath. Never had she seen such frank desire in a man's eyes—or at least felt so physically affected by it. Suddenly her skin felt hot and prickly.

"Will you have dinner with me tonight? I know a little Serbian place—"

"I can't, Giulio. I have a pile of work to do this afternoon—"

His hand covered hers, and the tingling that began in her fingertips raced up her arm and down her spine. "Mama Radicevic makes cevapcici and burek you could cry over—"

"And I'll need a nap before we start shooting tonight—"

"And her sarma—"

"You're incorrigible!" Kate laughed.

"A raincheck, then?"

Kate looked at his hand, which was still sheltering hers. It felt warm and dry and very strong. "Yes, a raincheck."

Seemingly reluctant to release his grasp, Giulio gestured for their lunch tab, settled their bill, and led Kate from the restaurant and back into the sunshine.

"It's a glorious day." Kate sighed. The sun was soothing on her shoulders, and her wayward senses made her feel that the warmth from Giulio's hand was beginning to envelop her entire body.

Giulio signaled vainly at an approaching taxi. "Which way are you going? Can I drop you?"

"No, thanks. I'm only a couple of blocks from here—up Eighth and over one."

"In that case"—he tucked her arm tightly beneath his—"I'll walk you," he announced, grinning mischievously.

"Summer's coming," Kate attempted conversationally. She sniffed then sniffed again. "I could swear I smell lilacs. Do you smell lilacs?"

"In midtown Manhattan?"

Kate sniffed again, but the scent had been replaced by another—an attar of the deep forest, yet pungent and sealike. Slowly she turned her head from left to right. The scent was Giulio's, and it was delicious.

As they neared her corner, he said, "When was the last time you took an afternoon off, just for the hell of it?"

She tried to pull away from him so that she could look up into his eyes, but he gripped her arm so tightly she couldn't. "I can't remember," she admitted. It sounded awfully lame, but it was true.

"Then we're going to Central Park."

"But—"

"And no *buts*." He threaded them through a knot of taxis blocking Fifty-sixth Street.

"Now just a minute—" she began. Then she caught his scent again, and it seemed to prickle her nose and dive straight down to some secret place deep inside her.

"Hmm?"

"To the park, to the park."

"I don't think anyone went back to work today," Kate acknowledged when they reached their destination. Every bench was occupied, the paths were filled with strollers, and fearless young men with rubber bands where their joints should have been practiced daring limbo routines on roller skates.

Giulio spread his jacket for her beneath a maple sapling, and she leaned against the trunk while he stretched out beside her, his head propped on his hand. Closing her eyes, she raised her face to the sun. Orange and yellow planets burst behind her eyelids, and the fist of tension that had been clenched between her shoulder blades slowly opened. "Hmm. Very nice."

Her eyes blinked open at the sound of hoarse panting as two runners threw themselves on the grass a few yards away. Sweat streamed down their arms and legs, and droplets clung to the tips of their noses. One was hollow-cheeked, slat-legged, and, to Kate's surprise, a woman. The man was baby-fat chubby and glistened like butter.

"Hu–Huu–Harvey," wheezed Slats, "how am I going to make you into a runner?" Her voice slid upward in a skid of despair. "The marathon is only six months from now."

Harvey licked his lips and moaned poignantly. "What does it matter? In twenty minutes I'll be dead of terminal shin splints."

"Let's go, Harve," Slats ordered, pulling the reluctant Harvey to his feet. "You're going to be healthy if it kills you." She loped down the path with Harvey trotting painfully after.

Giulio shook his head. "I think they're doomed, don't you?"

"Do you know what shin splints are? Or is it impolite to ask?"

"It's an inflammation here," Giulio said, stroking his thumb along her shin. She checked an inward shiver. "I don't think you need to worry." He stroked it again, examining her leg with great care. "An excellent specimen."

Her leg tingled from hip to toe. "I'm relieved to hear it." She grinned and nervously recrossed her ankles. "I'll remember that if I decide to join the shorts-and-sweat crowd."

Laughing, he rolled onto his back, nestling his head

in Kate's lap. The casual but intimate gesture gave the tingling that had begun in Kate's leg a new locus. Giulio breathed a long, contented "Ahhh!" and closed his eyes.

What was she doing, lounging in the park in the middle of the afternoon with this—this—randy Italian's head in her lap, Kate wondered. She was supposed to be home working. She had a shoot at midnight, heaven help her. So why was she here? Because Giulio Fraser wanted someone to amuse him for an afternoon, that was why. How had she let herself get bulldozed into this? She must have been out of her mind. In a couple of minutes she would get up and go home . . .

But the warming sun soothed her, and Giulio's steady breathing lulled her. The grass was newly mown, the earth yeasty with the mingled smells of new buds, new greenery, and quickening life. How heavy his head was, she thought. Even in the sunlight his black hair was as shadowless as velvet. Cautiously Kate slipped a probing finger into the center of an ebony curl. His hair was springy, coarse as sea wrack, and it smelled excitingly of spindrift. For an irrational instant she allowed herself to imagine those rough curls cradled against her breasts.

Drowsily his eyes opened, and he smiled up at Kate so knowingly that she shivered. He snuggled his ear against her stomach. "I can hear your lunch in here."

"Hmm?" She wound another curl around her finger.

"It's murmuring very politely in Japanese."

She heard the couple before she saw them—the woman's voice tight and thin with anger, the man's reedy with exasperation. The breeze carried their words away, leaving only a confused babble behind. Kate watched them find a bench just out of earshot. Both were blond with pale eyes and small hands, hers fluttering just above her lap, his clenched on his knees.

"That must be quite a fight," Giulio observed, sitting up. "What do you guess they're arguing about?"

"I think the real argument's over, and they've come to the making-up stage, but the husband's finding it harder to do."

"Husband? I don't think they're married. They're too— too—careful of each other. Husbands and wives can cut each other to ribbons with dull butter knives at ten paces."

"Have you been married?" she asked, wondering at the bitterness of his comment. It sounded like something *she* might say.

"No," he said, without taking his eyes from the couple on the bench. He suddenly looked at her. "You're not married, are you?"

"No," she said, rushing on before he could ask another question. "Well, whatever they are, they've known each other for a very long time. There! Did you see that? The way he reached for her hand? He didn't have to look for it—he knew where it would be. That means he's lived with her for years. They must be married. If you think about it, they even look a little bit alike, don't you think? Same facial structure, same coloring."

"No," he scoffed. "They're not at all alike. Look how different their expressions are. And there's a certain look in their eyes . . . they're definitely not married. They're lovers."

"You wanna bet?"

"You're on!" he said, taking her hand and pulling her to her feet.

"What are you going to do?"

"Eavesdrop. Be casual." Hand in hand they sauntered over behind the bench and with elaborate nonchalance seated themselves on the hill just behind the couple. Without warning Giulio wrapped Kate in his arms.

"What are you doing?" Kate protested in a whisper.

"Spying. Pretend you're 007," he breathed into her ear.

Giggles clogged her throat. "And what are you doing in the middle of Central Park, sir, with your arms around James Bond? *You* can be James Bond; I'll be Miss Marple."

"Shh!" He nibbled on her earlobe. "Pretend we're lovers."

It was deliciously easy to manage that, she silently acknowledged. She was powerless to keep her body from melting into his as his lips explored her ear.

The woman on the bench was saying, "I think she should have married him. I'd marry him tomorrow if he asked me."

"See?" Giulio hissed, squeezing her shoulder. "They're not married."

"There you go again," said the man. "One kiss and you'd follow him anywhere. You're not a fighter, Paula. You're a wimp."

"You're right," Kate whispered, "but they don't sound like lovers, either."

"Well," said the woman, "I think Jill Clayburgh is certifiably nuts! I wouldn't let Alan Bates get away— even if he was an artist. And just because you're my brother—"

"Oh, no!" Giulio moaned, sputtering with laughter and pulling Kate to the ground.

"Oh, yes!" Kate chortled, digging him in the ribs. "They're fighting over a movie. Now don't make me laugh out loud." She buried her face in his shirt. "And you, James Bond, don't think they look at all alike."

His chest heaved with suppressed laughter, and he gave her ribs a relentless squeeze. Kate crammed his tie against her mouth, but the tighter he held her, the more she shook with silent laughter, until her ribs ached and her lungs burned. Just when she knew she couldn't last another second, they both burst out in a joyous, whooping, howling duet and lay, helpless with laughter, in each other's arms.

Paula leaped to her feet. "Look! Look!" her brother shouted, pointing at them angrily. "I've told you and I've told you. The city's full of crazy people!" The pale couple fled across the park.

Kate sat up, her chest heaving, tears running down her face. Giulio lay on his back, his arms outstretched, gasping for breath. Kate wiped her eyes, sniffing hard and trying not to start laughing again. The effort left her panting.

Flushed and hiccuping, Giulio sat up. "What have you done?" he demanded, holding up the twisted string that had been his tie.

"Let me have it." She swallowed a painful bubble of laughter. "I'll iron it for you."

He loosened the knot and yanked it off. "You shall have it as a memento, Marple."

"I shall always treasure it, 007." She gulped a brave tear. "But now I must fly. Duty calls."

"Must you, Marple?" he pleaded, one hand to his heart.

"I have a brochure to lay out before tiffin."

"Forget it." His face darkened, all laughter gone, his eyes as hard and opaque as coal. "I want you to have dinner with me."

Kate shook her head. "I can't." Shivery goose bumps prickled her arms. At his searching look, she emphasized, "Really."

Absently he stuffed his tie into his pocket. Kate tried

to read his eyes, but she could see only her reflection—twinned, doubled by black mirrors.

"Thank you for the lunch," she said, turning away from his stern demeanor.

"Have a good shoot," he shouted after her. When she looked over her shoulder, his eyes almost seemed to be dancing with laughter. Damn, but the man was contradictory!

Kate had just started laying out a complicated twelve-page brochure for a travel agency when Marion called.

"How about coming over for tuna casserole? It started out as a discrete dish for one, but I had a few things left over from the other night, so I threw those in. Now it's going to be enough for six."

"I'd love to, Marion, but I just decided to eat an apple and skip dinner. I had an enormous lunch. Lots of tuna, as a matter of fact. Giulio took me to lunch at Nomura's."

"He did?" Marion's voice was breathy with suspicion. "What did you eat?"

"All kinds of sushi and sashimi. It was all delicious; I'm afraid I ate like a pig."

"Kate Elliot! Do you realize that fish was raw?"

"You must be kidding."

"I most certainly am not. What you had on your rice was raw fish. I've read about it."

"Well, there's no reason to sound scandalized. Nothing that tastes that good could possibly be bad for you. I refuse to think about it. Tell me what's going on at the foundation."

"The usual, only more so. I'm knee deep in reports, and the boss man is flying off to a conference in Los Angeles. By the time he gets back, I may find the top of my desk again. I haven't seen it since last Christmas—

I don't even remember if it's wood or Formica. Are you sure you won't come over?"

"I really can't."

"Do you still think Fraser is opinionated, stubborn, and all those other things?"

"I guess I'm having second thoughts. He was so different today—caring and sort of..." *Beguiling* was the word that came to mind, but she didn't say it. How could she explain their gloriously ridiculous afternoon in the park? It was not to be shared with anyone else—at least not yet. "Maybe food tames the savage beast or something. I've never met anyone, man or woman, who cared so passionately about food. And at the same time he has this weird streak of fantasy."

"Why weird?"

"It's so unexpected—at least *I* didn't expect it. Everyone has a little streak, but his is about a mile wide and a foot deep."

"What did you two do, for heaven's sake?" Marion sounded alarmed again.

Kate laughed. "We just fooled around."

"You sound like Fraser's beginning to get to you."

"Don't be ridiculous."

CHAPTER FIVE

THE GYM LOOKED huge and hollow. Rings and bars hung motionless from the high ceiling. Islands of exercise mats were clustered here and there on the hardwood floor. Three complex exercise machines, all of fiercely gleaming chrome with steel pulleys, lurked menacingly at one end of the room, while racks of dumbbells squatted nearby. Kate was surprised to discover floor-length mirrors spaced at intervals on all the walls. The room was not unlike a dance studio, she decided, the light harsh and unforgiving. Their backs turned to their multiplying reflections, Jeffrey, the photographer Melissa Edwards, and her assistant huddled around a small table drinking coffee.

Kate was always curious to discover how people revealed themselves by what they wore when they really got down to work. Last year she had illustrated a children's book for a man who was immaculately turned out in his publisher's office but who wrote, she had discovered to her dismay, in nothing but a ratty old bathrobe and a three-day growth of beard.

Having long ago learned that photo sessions were invariably hot, sweaty, and grubby for the art director, she had worn jeans, a pale green T-shirt, and a lavender baseball cap to keep the glaring lights from her eyes. Jeffrey wore baggy corduroy trousers and a fuzzy yellow sweater. The man he was talking with looked like a perfectly exposed print—all shades of gray and salt-and-pepper hair. Beside him stood an exquisite Eurasian woman, dressed, like Kate, in jeans and a tangerine T-shirt. An enormous coil of orange extension cord hung from her shoulder.

"Hi!" she said as Kate joined them. "I'm Melissa Edwards, and this is Simon—my husband, my partner, and today my assistant. Both our assistants are in bed with colds—"

"So I'm acting as Melissa's gofer," Simon concluded. "Have a doughnut."

So this is the famous team of Edwards and Edwards, Kate thought. She had admired Melissa's fashion photographs ever since her college days. Simon, she knew, specialized in product shots.

"Isn't this an awful time to start work?" said Jeffrey. "Have some coffee. We're waiting for Gunilla."

"No!" boomed a voice from the doorway. "Gunilla is here!" A Viking warrior-maiden in a blue track suit paced swiftly toward them. "Here, I have brought good food to sustain us." An Earth goddess showering them with her bounty, she brought forth from her mammoth carryall packets of raisins, nuts, figs, dates, and granola, pots of yogurt, a dozen oranges, and as many apples. "Melissa and Simon and Jeffrey I know. You must be Katrina," she said, looking down from what Kate estimated to be all of six feet. "How tiny you are—and too soft," she accused, kneading Kate's right arm. "I am ready. Shall we begin?"

"You're the one who'll be working from the photos, Kate, so I'll leave everything up to you and Melissa to work out," Jeffrey said. "I'll tick off each pose on the log as we go so we don't miss any."

"What about the cover photo?" Kate asked.

"When I see something I like, I'll shoot some color," Melissa replied.

With his clipboard on one knee, Jeffrey made himself comfortable and bit into a jelly doughnut.

"That is poison, Jeffrey," said Gunilla. "What doesn't go to your heart will go to your hips."

He licked his fingers, smiling sheepishly.

"Right," Kate said briskly. "Let's get to work. I'd like to start with your floor exercises, Gunilla." She walked to the matted area she had chosen. "Simon, drop your background paper here, please, just at the edge of the mat. When you've set your lights, we'll cut the ceiling fluorescents. Melissa, what do you think of using a key spot to bring out the musculature in relief?"

"Fine," Melissa agreed, snaking another cord across the floor.

"Gunilla, take your place please," Kate directed.

Watching Gunilla strip to her leotard and tights, Kate saw how right Giulio was. Her body was so perfect she would have intimidated Michelangelo.

"I'd like to wet down that fabric so that it really clings, Gunilla. I hope you don't mind," said Kate.

"Whatever you say," the Valkyrie replied, raising her arms to shoulder height so that Simon could wet her down. He had brought a spray bottle containing glycerin and water, and the process took several minutes, there was such a lot of Gunilla.

"It tickles, Simon. Haw!" She rumbled a vast, Viking giggle as he sprayed down one side of her rib cage.

"Can you tie your hair back?" Melissa asked. "It's hiding your neck."

Gunilla padded dutifully to her carryall and, rummaging through it, came up with a red shoelace and lashed it around her great sheaf of yellow hair.

Hour after hour they worked. The only sounds were the steady whiz-chunk, whiz-chunk, of Melissa's camera shutter, and gentle thumps as Gunilla changed positions. Kate and Melissa occasionally discussed camera angles; Simon moved lights, adjusted the white umbrella reflectors, changed bulbs, and reloaded Melissa's second camera so that she could shoot without pause.

Gunilla ran effortlessly through the routines that would transform more mortal women into mini-Vikings—or at the very least work off their "love handles." She took such obvious pleasure in her exercises, in her body's suppleness and strength, that after the first fifteen minutes Kate was filled with affectionate admiration for her.

At five in the morning they broke for a rest. Simon made a fresh pot of coffee and opened a picnic hamper full of roast beef sandwiches. Gunilla munched granola.

When they went back to work, Melissa shot some color and then went back to black and white. Late in the morning Kate suddenly realized that Giulio was standing outside the glare of the lights, behind Jeffrey's chair, watching her. How long, she wondered, has he been standing there? His unannounced presence both excited and jarred her; she felt oddly exposed.

"Break, everybody!" she called. Her shirt was soaked through, and she could see that Gunilla, too, was stream-

ing sweat from both the lights and the exertion. It was
chilly now with the lights switched off. Kate shivered
and pulled her jacket around her shoulders. Giulio instantly handed her a cup of hot coffee.

"You really know what you're doing, Marple." He
grinned.

"I ought to by now," she snapped. How patronizing
he sounded. Had he thought she was an amateur?

"Hey, simmer down. Don't be cranky. I'm impressed.
You're a good art director."

"I'm not cranky. I'm sorry I barked. It's been a very
long morning, and I'm tired, sweaty... and cranky."

"I missed you at dinner last night. Did you finish your
brochure?"

"Just barely. I had to work like a maniac until it was
time for the shoot. I only stopped for five minutes to eat
an apple."

Giulio looked stricken. "That was your dinner—an
apple?" His hands closed over her shoulders, and he
shook her gently. "What am I going to do with you,
Kate?"

"You'll just have to take me as I am, sir." She laughed.

"Oh, I will, Kate, I will." His eyes flashed black fire.
"Could you do this again tomorrow?" he suddenly asked.

"But we're nearly finished here."

"No, I mean with me. Simon is going to shoot some
Georgian silver for me tomorrow, and I want you to be
there. Are you booked?"

"No, as a matter of fact I'm clear for two days."

"Splendid," he said, grinning. "Meet me at the Edwards' studio at nine. And when you finish here, get
some sleep. That's an order. I don't want you cranky."

He reached out and pulled the bill of her cap down to her nose. "See you tomorrow."

Before she could speak, he had turned away and was walking toward the door with his arm around Jeffrey's shoulder, laughing as he went.

"Does he make fun of you?" asked Gunilla, munching a handful of nuts. "I think there is more there than fun. *Ja?*"

"'I *want* you to be there . . . That's an *order,*'" Kate mimicked. "Who does he think he is?"

"He is your boss, yes?"

"Not for any book on Georgian silver. Yours is the only one I've contracted for."

Gunilla lifted one perfect eyebrow in a golden arc. "Then why did you agree to go?"

"You know, I'm honestly not sure." She finished her coffee. "He's very hard to say no to."

Gunilla offered her some nuts and looked skeptical. "And very attractive?"

Kate winced. "Okay, back to work," she called to the others. "We're almost done."

She was so tired she felt punchy and stiff. Melissa and Simon groaned. Sighing, Jeffrey bent over his clipboard. Gunilla, fresh as ever, bounded back to her place on the mat and picked up her ten-pound dumbbells.

When at last they were finished and Gunilla had pulled on her track suit, kissed everyone good-bye, and trotted off, Kate helped Melissa and Simon roll up all their bright orange cords and disassemble their lights.

As they walked together to the elevator, Jeffrey put his arm around Kate in a comfy hug. "That was one helluva good shoot, my dear. Giulio asked you to be with him to shoot the Georgian silver cover, didn't he?"

Kate nodded.

"Good. If it goes well tomorrow, he'll probably offer you that book, too. I suspect he has visions of turning you into his assistant."

"But I've already told him I'm not interested in giving up my accounts to work for him. Besides, don't you want to be his assistant?"

"Not in this life!" he boomed. "I'm a designer, period. It may come as something of a surprise to you, my dear, but inside every designer there is not necessarily an art director fighting to get out. However, in you—in you I think he sees one."

"And hasn't the great man ever been wrong?"

"Not within living memory, my dear."

CHAPTER SIX

THE EDWARDS' STUDIO was in a narrow, three-story brick house on East Eighteenth Street. The windows were tall but few, and the house seemed so unlikely a place for a commercial studio—so withdrawn and residential, so privately domestic—that Kate checked the address twice before she rang. Simon opened the door almost instantly.

"This way," he greeted her cheerfully, leading her through a door at the back of a tiny outer office. She stepped into a world of light. The entire ground floor had been turned into a huge, high-ceilinged studio. The back wall, facing the garden, had been replaced entirely by glass. Movable floodlights hung from a metal grid high up under the black-painted ceiling. Dozens of lamp stands were clustered in serried ranks. A deep wooden rack, built like a honeycomb, held a rainbow of colored background papers.

"The lab's over there," he said, pointing to a small

room built into one corner of the studio.

"Who lives upstairs?" she wondered aloud.

"We do. Bedrooms upstairs, kitchen downstairs. We had to sacrifice the living room and dining room to make the studio, but they were no great loss. The kitchen's plenty big for all of us to eat in and then some." Taking Kate's arm, he walked her around the perimeter of the studio. "Waiting for client approval before I tear them down," he said, gesturing toward several different objects that had been set up to be photographed and now sat abandoned.

She paused to admire a shallow earthenware bowl resting on a teakwood stand. "It's beautiful, Simon. Is it Sung dynasty?"

"Yes, you've got it in one. Twelfth century, Korea. It's going to be the cover, I hope, for a gallery mailing. There's not much money in gallery work, but it surely does feed the soul. It's a great change from industrial bearings and wallpaper . . . I wonder where Giulio is. That man is never late."

"Where's Melissa?"

"She'll be back soon. The twins finally finished their papier-mâché model of Mont-Saint-Michel, so she took them to school in the van with the thing—complete with Benedictine abbey—in the back. It took all four of us to get it in there," he said with a laugh. "You're sure to meet the kids when they get home from school—they're always in here when we're working. They're both camera crazy," he said proudly. "Rick and Polly. Twelve years old."

All this and two kids, Kate thought. Melissa's certainly one woman who's managed to combine her marriage with a successful career. Of course their photography was obviously very much a family affair. That shared understanding was probably what made it all possible.

On a bright trill of Melissa's laughter, she and Giulio burst into the studio. He cradled a parcel in his arms—a bulky lump wrapped in newspapers and a ragged grocery bag.

"Tell them," Melissa said as she giggled at Giulio. "Tell them."

Giulio wiped his eyes, composing his face into a mask of great seriousness. He cleared his throat solemnly but winked surreptitiously at Kate. "I went to the author's apartment this morning to collect this"—he patted his disreputable parcel—"and he insisted on coming along for the shoot. He's a dreadful old fidget; he'd drive us absolutely crazy. So I looked him straight in the eye and said, in the most sepulchral voice I could muster, 'Have you had mumps?'

"'No, never,' said he, and his eyes opened wide like a startled rabbit's.

"'Then you dare not come,' said I. 'Mumps contracted after puberty can leave you sterile. The Edwards' twins have mumps.' I left him standing in his hall looking like a man who'd narrowly escaped death. Oh, Kate, I wish you'd been there."

"You're terrible!" she said, laughing.

"Giulio, that's rotten," said Simon with a hoot of laughter. "Absolutely rotten, but I love it! Is that the pot? In that awful bag?"

"Sure. I'd be asking to be mugged if I carried it around New York in its fitted case. I'll need some cotton film gloves, please, Simon."

He peeled away the layers of newspaper to reveal a neatly tied white paper package. When this was unwrapped he pulled on the gauzy white gloves and, like a magician, produced a blue flannel bag tied with blue ribbons. From the bag he extracted a silver coffee pot with a faceted, swan-necked spout and dark, boxwood handle.

They all spoke at once. "It's beautiful." "Gorgeous." "Magnificent."

"Yes," Giulio said, the word hissing slowly out on a long exhalation of breath as he turned the pot for them to admire. It was elegant and graceful, its cylindrical body curving in to form the base and molded foot. The silver shone richly with a luminous gray luster. "I want you to shoot it two ways, Simon—first with a white tent and then against a black background."

Together Simon and Melissa created a white tent over a table so Simon could photograph the pot without any errant reflections disfiguring its gleaming silver surface. Once the lights were painstakingly set within the tent, Giulio and Simon took turns peering into the massive studio camera, the lens of which peeked through a hole cut in the white paper.

"Anything showing?" Giulio asked Simon, who was crouched behind his camera, staring into the ground glass back.

"Everything, dammit! Come look."

Giulio, joining him behind the camera, uttered what Kate took to be an ancient Italian malediction. Melissa caught her eye, and they grinned at each other. While Giulio and Simon conferred behind the camera, Melissa and Kate slithered through the two-foot gap between the bottom of the tent and the floor and moved the lights as directed. They moved them up and down. They moved them to the right, to the left, and back to the right again.

"It's hideous!" said Giulio, and he backed away to let Simon take his place.

Kate rolled her eyes, and Melissa muttered, "Silver is always a bitch to shoot. It's worse than cut crystal."

"The handle needs more light," said Simon. "It looks like a dead twig. And I've lost the curve of the belly above the base."

"And I saw a lamp stand on the spout," Giulio complained. "You two watch this time. We'll try to move the lights."

So Kate and Melissa stood with their heads together behind the camera. "You need some more light on the base," Melissa said.

"And a little less on the dome," added Kate.

Finally Giulio and Melissa and Kate agreed that the pot looked right.

"I know I'm going to hate it," said Simon.

"Let's shoot a Polaroid anyway," said Giulio, "just to see what we've got."

A few minutes later they all crowded around to look at the print.

"It's close," said Kate, hoping her voice didn't betray her disappointment. The base was much too dark, and the whole thing lacked sparkle.

"I hate it," Simon grumbled. "It looks like a reject from a Confederate mess kit."

"Cheer up, kids," Giulio said. "Now we know where we're heading. I'm going to go pick up some lunch for us, and then we'll get back to it."

Simon stumped off to the darkroom, muttering to himself.

"You mustn't mind Simon," Melissa said. "He's always grumpy when he's working. He's never satisfied. Of course, Giulio's never satisfied either, so they make a great pair."

Kate helped Melissa clear off the top of a low cabinet. From inside it Melissa brought out plates, silverware, and glasses.

"We have a lot of working lunches here," she explained. "Also dinners and sometimes even breakfasts. This saves running downstairs to the kitchen. And I insisted on this built-in refrigerator—I have fashion models who subsist entirely on celery juice, cottage cheese, and air."

"Is it really true that they have their back teeth pulled so that their cheeks will look hollow?"

"Some few still do. But that look's going out, and those who were born with good cheekbones don't need it."

"Hey, give me a hand, Kate," Giulio called from the doorway, instantly commandeering her into helping him unpack his groceries. "Come on, Simon, lunch," he yelled.

He had brought several salads, slices of pâté, a smoked Italian cheese, two skinny loaves of French bread, a chilled bottle of Orvieto, and some oranges.

When they had filled their plates, Simon and Melissa excused themselves and went together to the front office, pleading paperwork. Giulio mounded Kate's plate with an assortment of the delicacies, then made a duplicate arrangement for himself.

As she popped a piece of cheese into her mouth, Giulio's voice brought her up short.

"Tell me, what do you do with yourself when you're not working?"

She swallowed before answering, "I draw whenever I can find some free time. Someone—Goya, I think—said if a man falls from a second-story window, an artist should be able to characterize him before he hits the ground. I still have a long way to go by those standards, but I'm working on it. I draw in Central Park when the weather's good."

"You're very serious, aren't you? What else do you do?" he probed.

"I'm writing and illustrating a children's book. It's a very spooky story, based more or less on some of the old Norwegian folk tales my grandmother used to tell me. It's full of monsters and scary forests. May I have some more of the pasta salad, please?"

He handed her the carton. "But when you're not honing your skills or working on your book, what do you do to relax? Are you going with anyone?" he questioned relentlessly.

"No, I'm not seeing anyone just now," she said hesitantly, thinking somewhat guiltily of Neal's unfulfilled wish for a romantic liaison with her.

"Ah hum. You've broken up recently? Why?"

She shook her head. This was really none of his business. She certainly didn't want to discuss Neal's persistent but fruitless pursuit of her. "Tell me—" she began, but he broke in, ignoring her question.

"Why?" he persisted.

The man was exasperating! "If you must know, I didn't break up with Neal, because there was nothing to break up. He's so much like my ex-husband—"

Giulio coughed into his wineglass. "Ex-husband?" He cleared his throat, swallowing hard. "I thought you said—"

"I said I wasn't married; I didn't say I hadn't been."

"You should have been a lawyer." It was his turn to sound exasperated. "And what about this Neal?"

"Neal's a friend who wants to be more than a friend— a romance that never happened, that's all."

Giulio looked relieved. "Ah, hum. Why didn't it?"

"Neal's both dependent and domineering—that's a terribly destructive combination."

"You don't believe a man should dominate his woman?" It was both a question and a flat assertion. His eyes had been deadly serious, but now something in the way he pursed his lips reminded her of their gloriously silly afternoon in the park. She knew she would have to know him much better before she could tell with any certainty whether he was serious or playing games with her. At the moment she sensed that he was doing both.

"That's the key, isn't it—*his* woman—like his chair or his rug. No, that's not what I think a relationship should be." She tossed her head angrily and rapped on the chair arm for emphasis. "It's certainly not what *I* want!"

He made no answer, but stretching out his long legs, he tilted his chair back at a dangerous angle and tugged thoughtfully on his earlobe, studying Kate with half-closed eyes. "You're feisty, aren't you? You have what we call *temperamento.*" He laughed. He suddenly righted his chair, and slowly, with far more care and deliberation than the task demanded, he stripped the peel from two oranges, dividing the sections between their two plates. "Dessert," he said, smiling.

Carrying her plate with her, Kate walked over to the Sung bowl. How she envied Simon and Melissa, working together without strain, supportive of one another, creating together. How different their backgrounds must be, and yet how perfectly they fit each other, with a gentle reciprocity. That was what she wanted, too, she reflected—a relationship of two equals sharing their love, sharing their life, but spiritually free—free to create, free to work. It must be possible to have love and security and freedom all at the same time. Melissa and Simon certainly seemed to know the secret. She idly wondered if Simon had a brother who wasn't spoken for.

"A penny for them," Giulio said quietly. She had scarcely heard him come up behind her.

"I was thinking of what a perfect relationship Melissa and Simon have." She didn't mind admitting him that far into her thoughts.

"It has been for the last eight years, and I'm sure it will continue to be. They seem very solid now, but it's no secret to their friends that their first years of marriage were rocky. They very nearly separated more than once."

"I can't believe it, seeing them now."

"True, though. Melissa had already made quite a name for herself as a fashion photographer when they decided to get married, but Simon was still struggling along. If it's hard for a man to accept the fact that his wife is more successful than he when they're in different fields, it's ten times harder when they're competing in the same field. It took a long time for Simon to admit to himself that he was never going to make it in fashion. When he discovered that his real talent lay in fine art and product shots, the conflict was over. You can't make a marriage with two rivals—it poisons the relationship."

"Yes, I expect it does," she said.

Suddenly he chuckled. "Remember *The Taming of the Shrew?* Katherine submitted to Petruccio in the end."

"Do you really think so? Katherine set her own limits, after all. I've always imagined that the two of them went on roistering through life together, surrounded by a flock of laughing, noisy children."

"You may be right, Kate, you may be right." His eyes had turned darkly serious, but the corners of his mouth were turning upward in a gentle smile.

CHAPTER SEVEN

IT WAS LATE afternoon before all the lighting problems
had been solved and Simon was sufficiently satisfied to
take his series of pictures and turn them over to their lab
man for processing. Just as he stepped out of the darkroom, the twins hurtled into the studio.

"Hi, Uncle Giulio," they called. "Whatcha got?" They
raced to the paper tent and dropped to the floor to peek
under it.

"*Uncle* Giulio?" Kate queried.

"I'm their godfather," he said, grinning.

"Manners," Melissa warned in a low voice, and the
twins slid sheepishly from beneath the tent to be introduced to Kate. They were breathtakingly beautiful children, Kate saw, favoring their mother, with blue-black
hair, enormous eyes, and heart-shaped faces. Rick wore
a Yankee baseball jacket, Polly a jockey's jacket of crim-
son-and-white checked silk.

"If those shots are keepers, Simon," said Giulio, "I'd

like to go right on and do the black background shots tonight. Would you mind?"

"You're the boss," Simon replied.

"Then why don't you two stay for dinner?" Melissa suggested. "Your stuff won't be out of the processor for an hour."

"We wouldn't want to trouble you," Kate said.

"It's no trouble, believe me. I'll just go tell Mrs. Wing," said Melissa. "Do you like spicy food, Kate?"

"If she didn't before, she does now," Giulio said with a laugh. "I gave her lunch at Mohan's."

"Mrs. Wing cooks everything but breakfast," piped Rick. "She likes to sleep in."

"And she cleans everything," Polly added, "but we have to make our own beds."

"I see," said Kate.

"Mother says Mrs. Wing is her treasure," Polly continued. "Mother says a woman with children and a husband and a career—"

"That's enough, Polly," Simon cut in.

"Would you like to see our pictures, Miss Elliot?" Rick asked. "C'mon upstairs. We have lots of new ones, Uncle Giulio." Tugging and urging, the twins hurried Kate and Giulio up the stairs.

"This is our studio," Polly announced proudly to Kate. "Daddy even built us our own darkroom in the hall closet."

There were twin worktables in the center of the room, and low shelves held the children's clutter of cameras, lens cases, bags, and lights. Two adjoining walls were completely covered with prints, one wall for Rick, the other for Polly.

"We've gotten better, haven't we?" Rick prompted Giulio.

"Hm," he said. "Let me look."

Rick's wall was an homage to speed and bodies in motion: there were graceful roller skaters in Central Park, twirling ice skaters in Rockefeller Center, riders crouched over racing bikes, leaping basketball players, twisting bodies straining at the moment of maximum effort.

Giulio let out a long, low whistle. "Hey, I like these, Rick," he said softly.

Polly's wall was devoted entirely to pictures of elderly men and women who had found a moment of rest and comfort. She had captured them sitting on stoops in the sun, playing chess in a park, walking with a grandchild's hand in each of theirs. How curious, Kate thought. In the very center of the wall, with all the pictures arranged around it, was a large color print of a white-haired woman asleep in a porch swing. A boy curled beside her in sleep, his head resting on her thigh. They had been shelling peas. With a start Kate realized the boy was Rick.

The two sleeping figures were caught in a timeless afternoon of dappled green shade. The picture glowed with serenity. Kate could feel the warm air, heavy and lazy. She could hear the tree toads humming in the woods. Placed as it was, with all the other pictures around it, this image of the old woman took on the power of an icon, a shrine. Kate felt strangely moved suddenly, and she glanced at Giulio standing close beside her. He must have felt it too; his hand sought hers and tightened around it.

"That's Grandma Edwards," Polly said at last. "Mummy took that the summer before she died."

"And that's me," Rick said. "Since Grandma Edwards died, Polly's taken pictures of nothing but old people. I think she's trying to work it through, don't you?"

"I don't need to work through anything, you big poop.

Old people are a lot more interesting than a bunch of nerds skating all over the park."

"That shows how much you know—"

"C'mon now, kids," Giulio interrupted. "Polly, your work is getting better all the time. You're both doing beautifully."

Rick was the first to regain his composure. "When we finish school," he said to Kate, "we're going to put up a sign out front." He looked at his sister to give her her cue, and they sang out together, "Edwards and Edwards and Edwards and Edwards."

"I'm going to do studio portraits and maybe some fashion stuff, and Rick's going to do sports, naturally," said Polly.

"Dinner in twenty minutes," Melissa called up the stairs. "Kids, wash your hands." The twins raced from the room and clattered down the stairs as Melissa appeared in the doorway. "Would you two like to come down for a drink? Mrs. Wing is asking for you, Giulio."

"Then we'd better get right down there," he said, slowly releasing Kate's hand. They all proceeded to the kitchen.

Mrs. Wing was a tiny Chinese woman with a face like a smiling walnut. Wisps of gray hair escaped from a bun at the back of her head, and beads of perspiration glistened on her forehead. She shook Kate's hand and grinned impishly at Giulio.

"Your lady?" she asked him bluntly.

"My colleague, Mrs. Wing," he corrected.

"You are the guest of honor," she said, patting Kate's arm. "You must sit there, across from Simon, Miss Colleague." She smirked at Giulio and, laughing to herself, turned back to her stove to fill the last serving dish before joining them at the big round table.

One platter held crescent-shaped fried dumplings; another, succulent slices of beef spiced with onions and hot peppers; a third brimmed with mixed greens and shredded chicken. At each place was set a bowl of rice and another of chicken broth with bean curd.

"Don't be shy, Kate," Simon urged. "Just reach."

So Kate joined in with the rest of the family and, holding her rice bowl in one hand, she selected morsels from each dish in turn, eating them with her rice as she went. It struck her as a very friendly way to eat, like holding a conversation with the others without actually talking.

"How are your assistants doing with their colds?" Giulio asked. "When do you think you'll have them back?"

"Monday, we hope," said Melissa.

"Mrs. Wing's been making them chicken soup," said Rick. "Polly and I deliver it."

"Mrs. Wing says chicken soup is Chinese penicillin," Polly announced.

Mrs. Wing giggled.

"May we be excused?" Rick asked. Like children everywhere, they ate with enormous speed, Kate observed.

"Have you finished your rice?" Melissa challenged.

"Yes," they chorused.

Melissa turned to Kate. "When I was growing up, my mother always said that if I didn't eat my rice I would marry an ugly man who'd beat me. As you can see, I never left a grain." She smiled fondly at Simon, who reached over to pat her hand.

"Okay, kids," said Melissa. "Homework. No television until you're done."

"Oh, Mom," they wailed in unison.

"Off you go," said Simon.

"It was nice meeting you, Miss Elliot," said each twin in turn.

"Thank you for showing me your pictures," Kate responded with a smile.

"Buona notte, zio Giulio," they said.

"Ciao, ragazzi," he replied, and the three of them laughed at what seemed to be some private joke of long standing.

When they had finished eating and Mrs. Wing had insisted Kate finish the one remaining dumpling, she brought them steaming hot towels and another pot of tea. Giulio fussed over her, telling her she was the finest Chinese cook in the world. "You are the pearl of the Orient," he declared.

Mrs. Wing laughed hugely and kissed him on both cheeks.

What a comfortable family, Kate thought. What inexhaustible goodwill. How effortlessly they had fit her into a place at their table and made her feel at home.

Simon and Giulio excused themselves and climbed the stairs to the studio. Mrs. Wing cleared the dishes from the table and carried them to a dishwasher in the scullery as Melissa poured them each another cup of tea.

"I know this is going to sound like I'm gushing," said Kate, "but this has been one of the happiest dinners I've ever had."

Melissa sighed. "They're a blissful family."

"I know a lot of women who would like to know how you've done it—combined your marriage, your children, and your career, and made it work."

"We made one helluva mess of it the first few years. It was Giulio who brought us back together. He's a very giving man, Kate, a truly loving friend. When we were first married, we went through a couple of years when my assignments were getting better and better while Simon's were getting worse and worse. We both started out in fashion; did you know that?"

"Yes," said Kate.

"You know as well as I do that there's no secret to being a good photographer—it's all a matter of knowing how to see. Anyone can learn the mechanics of handling cameras and lenses and lights. The magic or talent or whatever you want to call it is in how you see the subject—how your vision differs from the next guy's. And fashion is a very specialized field. I see a model one way, Hiro and Penn would see her their way. We use the same cameras, the same film—"

"But each of your visions is unique."

"Exactly."

"It's the same in illustrating or painting," Kate commented.

"Of course it is. Well, Simon's images were never distinctive, never his own—they were a pastiche of everyone else's. He just didn't have the eye for fashion shots, but it was a long and heartbreaking time before he finally accepted that fact.

"There we were, struggling along. I was flying off to crazy places like Marrakesh to shoot fashion spreads for *Vogue,* and Simon was shooting housedresses in New Jersey. It was awful. Then I got pregnant, and once the twins were born, my husband—who for the past nine months had been telling me how wonderful it was going to be to have children, how they would bind us together—my husband suddenly did a complete reversal. The children were taking up too much of my time and affection, and where did he fit in? And since I wasn't able to take on any assignments for a while, I was even more miserable."

"How did Giulio fit into all this?"

"He came over one night, and Simon and I started one of our awful fights. Giulio simply stood up and shouted us down. He told Simon he was acting like a jealous adolescent; he told me I was using the kids to avoid facing up to my feelings about Simon and my work."

"I'm not sure I understand what you mean."

"I loved Simon—I really did. It broke my heart to watch him beating his head against the wall of fashion work, and the better my assignments were, the guiltier I felt, because I was making it and he wasn't. And, Kate, I hated Simon for making me feel guilty. Somewhere deep inside I grew to despise him for doggedly, dumbly going on in a field where it was obvious to everyone he'd never make it. And I hated him for being jealous of the affection and time I gave my babies, and I hated myself for hating him."

"Didn't you resent Giulio's butting in like that?"

"Oddly enough, we didn't. He was telling us all the things we both needed desperately to hear, I guess—and secretly wanted to hear, too, I think. We needed to find a middle ground. And Simon just needed a good, strong shove in the right direction—he's brilliant at what he does. There isn't another photographer in New York who could make that silver pot of Giulio's look as gorgeous as Simon's shots will make it look."

"He knew how to see all along," said Kate.

"Of course he did. It was Giulio who helped him find his métier. He helped him get his first fine-art and product assignments. He also insisted I find myself a full-time, live-in housekeeper and cook and get back to work·instead of mooning around upstairs worrying about my stretch marks."

"Rick and Polly don't seem to have suffered because you went back to work," said Kate. "They're darling children. I think you've done a wonderful job with them, and Simon obviously adores them and dotes on you."

"I feel the same way about him. We were meant for each other—I really believe that—we just lost our way there for a while. We'll be grateful to Giulio for the rest of our lives for helping us find it again." Melissa paused. "I've been watching his eyes when he looks at you, Kate. He's seeing you as something more than a colleague, I think. Are you interested in him?"

"I'm not in his league, Melissa. This may sound silly to you, but I've known the name Fraser and admired his work since my very first design class, when he was one of the rising young stars of the design world. By the time I began working in New York, he had joined the company of the gods. I still find it terribly hard to separate the man from the legend. And even in person he's so much larger than life—so . . . commanding."

"Why do I get the feeling there's more to this than what you're saying?" Melissa probed.

Kate smiled. "Well . . . Melissa, I've never let myself get involved with a man I'm working for."

"It's not as though you're in the same office," she protested.

"Besides, I gather he's involved with Liz Madden."

"Is he really?" said Melissa. "And here I thought that was over years ago," she mused aloud. "Well, anyway, if you give Giulio a chance, you'll find he's quite like everyone else, only nicer."

Simon pushed open the kitchen door. "How much tea

can you two drink? C'mon, let's get back to work. Giulio says the white shots are keepers, and we're ready to start on the black background. We built the black tent while you two were gabbing and swilling tea."

The four worked steadily until midnight, adjusting lights and taking test shots. It was three in the morning before Giulio pronounced the transparencies perfect and Simon conceded, "They're not too bad."

Kate yawned. Putting his arm around her, Giulio said, "I'm taking this one home before she falls over."

She welcomed the warmth and strength of the encircling arm as they said their good nights to Melissa and Simon and made their way to the street. Giulio hailed a cab, and soon they were at Kate's building.

"Do you keep anything to drink in there?" Giulio questioned as Kate opened her apartment door.

"I have some Scotch. But, amazingly enough, I'm hungry again. I think I'll open a can of soup. Do you want some?"

"No, you go ahead. I can fix my own drink," he said, following her into her miniature kitchen. He cracked the tiny ice cube tray with the heel of his hand to pop it loose, then turned, tray in hand, looking for a place to set it down. "No wonder you don't cook," he said, dropping the tray into the sink. "This would be like cooking in a mailbox."

"It's big enough," she said, zipping the top off a soup can. "Cream of asparagus. Wouldn't you like some?"

He stood behind her, grimacing into the pot. Kate could feel his warm breath on the back of her neck as he spoke. "No, I'll leave you to it." He squeezed past her to walk around her living room, looking at her pictures.

"I like this," he said, peering at a drawing from her

student days. "This is very good."

"There are a lot of those Russian olive trees on the Minnesota campus," she said.

"Is that where you're from? Minneapolis?" He threw himself onto the couch, stretching his long legs beneath the coffee table.

Kate carried her soup bowl to a chair on the other side of the table. "Yes. My father's still there. He's a baker; my mother died when I was in college."

"And is that where you married?"

"Hmm. I was in my last year of school, and Jack was starting his law practice."

"And?"

"And nothing. It just didn't work, that's all."

He sipped his drink in thoughtful silence while Kate finished her soup. "Weren't you in love?"

Kate laughed, which seemed to startle him. "Oh, I was desperately in love. But I was in love with a dream."

Suddenly it was terribly important to her that Giulio understand. But how could he? He was so ineffably, so supremely male—so confident—she thought. There was no way he could understand a young girl's passionate hopes—or her terrors. He'd never had to struggle to keep from being stifled; he'd never fought to be independent. He couldn't understand a young woman's dreams. But wouldn't it be wonderful if he could?

He leaned toward her encouragingly.

"There were three of us who shared the same dreams. We built them together, a trio of starry-eyed carpenters. We were the Intrepid Trio, and we believed we could have everything: romance, love, marriage, career —and all at the same time. Nancy, Rebecca, and me . . . We were so sure we could do it." She shook her head ruefully. A thin film of soup was drying on the inside of the bowl; it looked like lichen growing in a shell.

"What happened to your Intrepid Trio?"

"Nancy went off to a Greek island to finish her novel and ended up marrying a vacationing dermatologist. She writes an occasional column for her PTA bulletin. Rebecca—Becky—drew like Botticelli. She married an engineer and works part-time drawing appliance ads for a discount store in La Jolla." She tried to swallow, but her mouth was too dry. "Failed dreamers, lost dreams." She laughed bitterly. "That would make a great song title, wouldn't it?"

"And what became of Kate?" His voice was gentle, and he turned his glass carefully in his fingers as if it were a piece of fruit, easily bruised.

"None of us had the marriage we dreamed of, and I'm the only one with the career and independence we all wanted so passionately."

"Why you, do you suppose?"

"Maybe I'm the only one who believed in it enough to fight for it. My mother exercised considerable influence in that area, actually. She was a very strong woman— teaching piano was her passion. She always said, 'It's a sin against God to waste your talent.' She really believed it, and she made me believe it."

"Your mother was right, Kate," he interrupted softly.

"I know she was," she responded. "So when I married Jack, I knew what our lives should be like. I had it all figured out ahead of time. Lawyer Jack would rise like cream to the top of his firm; he'd make partner in record time. And designer Kate would begin a brilliant career with a top local studio."

"But?" Giulio prompted quietly.

"But Jack didn't want me to work after I graduated.

He couldn't see why I needed to—that working creatively, professionally, was an important part of my life. You can't possibly imagine how disillusioning it is to discover that the person you love thinks your ambitions are trivial." She felt her pulse racing with remembered anger.

"I think you need a drink," said Giulio, rising and carrying his glass to the kitchen. "What did lawyer Jack expect you to do?" he called out.

"Keep house. Add another coat of wax to the kitchen floor. Paint flowers on trays . . . oh, I don't know."

Giulio returned and handed her a lethal-looking tumbler of Scotch and water. "Drink," he commanded. "I want to hear more. Drink. Think of it as Dutch courage."

Kate smiled. He did realize how important it was to her that he understand. She sipped her drink. It tasted like old, smoky logs, and it burned all the way down, but as the harshness subsided she felt some of her tension ease away with it. "Jack thought a working wife was *inappropriate*—his word. None of the other lawyers' wives worked. What would the partners say if I did?"

"They'd probably have said that Jack married a very talented and independent woman. It doesn't say much for us men, but it takes a very strong and giving man to love a strong and independent woman."

She looked up over the rim of her tumbler, breathing over the ice and fogging the glass. Absently she scribed a *G* on the glass and then hastily rubbed it off with her thumb. "It all came to a head when some friends of ours bought a nursery and landscaping business. I designed their logo and letterhead, and then I did their street signs and the delivery vans. I'd just begun working with the agency they'd chosen to do their ads when Jack put his foot down. 'What will the partners say? No wife of mine is going to work!'"

"Did you sit still for that?"

"I summoned up all my courage, and I told Jack I didn't give a damn what the partners thought. I told him that I was something more than a nifty combination sex-gratifying device and floor waxer, and that I intended to start free-lancing. If being a lawyer didn't prevent him from being a husband, then being a designer wouldn't prevent me from being a wife. I'd trained to be an artist and, dammit, I was going to be an artist!"

"What did he say?"

"Nothing you'd want to hear. We had one helluva fight." Restless and utterly drained, Kate crossed to the windows. The street below was empty, the northern sky washed pink and gold by a million neon signs. Morning would come soon, draining the pastels to gray just before dawn. "Soon after that I came to New York. What did I say? Failed dreamers, lost dreams?"

Giulio leaned back, clasping his hands behind his head. "Dreams are notoriously hard to kill, and you strike me as a very tenacious lady."

"You may be right," she murmured. "You just may be right." Smiling wryly to herself, she plucked her soup bowl from the coffee table, scrubbed it under the kitchen tap, and left it to drain. Humming softly, she returned the melting ice cubes to the freezer and wiped the counter. When she turned back to the living room, Giulio was stretched out on the couch, sound asleep.

She tiptoed through the room and returned with a pillow and the blanket from the foot of her bed. Carefully she pulled off his loafers. Gently she lifted his head to slip the pillow beneath it and was startled again by the exciting coarseness of his hair. He groaned in his sleep as she tucked the blanket around him. Tiny blue veins as fine as china crazing patterned his eyelids. Lightly she brushed a tangle of curls from his forehead, letting her fingers trail across his temple and over his cheek.

Still smiling, she turned out the lights and tiptoed to her bedroom. She left her door ajar and fell asleep listening to Giulio's deep, rhythmic breathing. It reminded her of the sea—slow waves breaking on a distant shore.

CHAPTER EIGHT

COFFEE, KATE THOUGHT. She smelled coffee. She was curled on her side, her arms wrapped around a pillow. Sunlight streamed across her bed. Squinting against the brightness, she peeped at her bedside clock. Ten-thirty! She clamped her eyes shut and pulled the covers up over her ears. Slowly the memory of yesterday's shoot and her early-morning talk with Giulio came back to her. She groaned. Whatever had possessed her to babble on like that about Jack, she wondered. Fatigue, she supposed.

Coffee. She did smell coffee. Giulio must still be there! Pulling on her robe, she peeked out her bedroom door.

He'd obviously showered. With a bath towel slung around his hips, he stood damply near-naked in her tiny kitchen, carefully peeling an apple.

Always the illustrator, Kate was pleased by the way the ceiling light threw his chest muscles into high relief.

As a professional, she relished his pectorals and his upper and lower abdominals. As a woman, she was tantalized by the blazon of black curls arrowing from his chest to his pelvis.

A long, thin spiral of apple peel hung suspended from his knife, a red and white spring uncoiling. Mesmerized, Kate watched the spring lengthen, simultaneously imagining Giulio's naked, hard-muscled body pressed against hers, his arms crushing her against him, while her hands . . . She caught her breath. She ached to touch him, to slide her exploring hands over those sharp ridges of muscle, fingering the clefts between . . .

He looked up, and she knew he could read the desire in her eyes. In his palm he held the moist white apple. Without taking his eyes from hers, his fingers closed around it, and he cupped it in his hand as he might cup a breast. Hypnotized, she stared as he raised it to his lips and licked away the juice collecting near his thumb.

She gasped, and he grinned over the apple. "Good morning," she croaked, her voice a nervous octave too high.

"Wonderful morning! Into the shower with you, Kate. The day's awasting."

"Are you always so bright and cheery in the morning? I was seriously considering sleeping until noon."

"Nonsense. First breakfast. Then I'm taking you shopping."

"Shopping? For what?"

"For dinner. I'm going to cook you a dinner such as you've never had before."

"You're not serious."

"Of course I am. I'm a brilliant cook, thanks to my mother. Now get dressed."

As she stood in the shower with the water bubbling

over her, Kate cautioned herself: *Be careful, girl—that is not a man to get involved with*. Despite what Melissa had said, Kate had no way of knowing for sure that Giulio wasn't still involved with Liz. They'd certainly seemed to be on intimate enough terms at Mohan's. And just because he'd been so nice and concerned last night was no reason to forget how imperious—and relentless—the great Fraser could sometimes be. Even in her befuddled emotional state, Kate suspected this was a relationship she would be wise to avoid. Don't even think about it, she commanded herself sternly.

But she did, in spite of herself. She soaped herself again, and she thought about his arms and his lips and his voice and his scent, and as she rinsed and stepped from the shower she thought: That man is turning me into the same kind of voluptuary he is. Toweling her hair dry, she regarded herself critically in the full-length mirror on the back of the bathroom door. Her legs were good, her hips slim. Her breasts were small, but they had a confident lift. You'll do, Kate, she thought. She winked impishly at her reflection.

Standing in front of her closet, she considered whether she would have a chance to get back and dress for dinner. Probably not. She'd have to wear something that was casual enough for shopping but good enough for the evening. She settled on an ivory silk blouse and a soft wool skirt and jacket the color of new moss.

Giulio was dressed when she got to the living room. He sat on the couch writing on a pad. "I've been making out our menu and shopping list. Your coffee's on the stove, and there's warm toast in the oven. You should be more careful about covering your butter, it tastes like onions." He went back to his list.

Kate munched her toast, thinking he was right. The

butter did taste of onions. He was lucky he hadn't had to eat it in January, when it tasted like herring. "Can you tell me what you're planning, or is it a surprise?"

"It's a surprise. Are you ready? First stop, Little Italy, then Soho, and we'll work our way back to my place."

Saturday shoppers thronged the sidewalks and spilled into the street. Shop doors stood open everywhere, and the air was pungent with roasting coffee and freshly baked bread. They passed fish markets, vegetable markets, meat markets, pasta shops, bakeries, and cafés, all echoing with chattering voices and laughter. Giulio guided her up the steps and through the nondescript entrance of a shop on Prince Street.

It looked as though all the shops in the neighborhood had been crammed into this one. The ceiling was festooned with a forest of sausages and ropes of onions and garlic. The shelves overflowed with everything Europeans had found worthy of bringing with them to America, with the heaviest emphasis on Italian products. Kate grew misty-eyed just reading the names of the places of origin on the beautifully ornate pasta boxes: Eboli, Modena, Abruzzi, Napoli, Bologna. She sighed. Next she discovered the two refrigerated cases that ran nearly the entire length of the store.

"Look, Giulio, quail eggs!" Beside them lay dressed quail and pheasants. In the next case she counted fourteen kinds of smoked fish and a dozen different kinds of dried mushrooms from France and Italy.

There were racks filled with pots and pans of every size, shape, and material; there were terrines, mills, brushes, spoons, servers, skimmers, kettles, and a copper fish poacher a yard long. There were tiny whisks the size of a finger and whisks as big as baseball bats. There were gleaming pasta machines and coffee pots.

Kate found baskets of fresh herbs, tied in little bundles that had been flown in from France. She discovered stuffed pastas from Italy. She was lost in contemplation of an olive-size pasta filled with fresh pumpkin when Giulio whispered in her ear.

"Your eyes are as big as saucers. You look like a kid at Christmas."

"What a wonderful place! Where do we start?"

"Cheeses. Over here," he urged. Turning to the man behind the counter, he requested the Gorgonzola. "Two pounds, please. That one looks good," he said, pointing to a blue-veined ivory wheel. "And a pound of Parmigiano Reggiano and a pound of Normandy butter." He chose some fresh fettuccine, selected some Greek olives, and then walked Kate around to the pastry case.

"Whatever you'd like, Kate. I leave it up to you."

There were jewellike tarts, cakes, and chocolate truffles. Kate glanced at Giulio. He was staring with unabashed longing at something labeled Le Nuage. "What's in that one?" she asked innocently.

"It's called 'The Cloud,'" he said dreamily, "It's apples poached in brandy and layered with crème fraîche between three whisper-thin leaves of pastry."

"Let's have it," she said. "You must have a sweet tooth the size of a fang."

"It runs in the family," he said airily.

At the vegetable market Kate pushed their cart through the crowded aisles while Giulio gave her a lecture on how to choose Romaine. He explained that he preferred California lemons to Florida lemons because they had more flavor and weren't too sweet.

He made a stop to buy three long, skinny loaves of French bread, each no thicker than Kate's wrist.

When the butcher at the meat market offered him something from the meat case, he shook his head, and the two of them fell into a vigorous discussion in Italian. Then the butcher disappeared into his meat locker and returned with a piece of meat so pale it looked like pink pearls.

"What are you buying?" said Kate.

"Milk-fed veal."

Kate carefully carried their boxed dessert, and Giulio carried everything else. He turned into West Eleventh Street—a tree-lined street of nineteenth-century houses and wrought-iron fences—and stopped at the walk to a two-story building of red-brown brick.

"This is my house," he said, juggling the bags in his arms and elbowing his jacket aside. He presented a jean-clad hip. "If you dig down in my pocket, you'll find my key." His jeans had been shrunk to fit, Kate noticed.

She tried to slide her fingers into his pocket, but it would have been easier to wedge her fingers into a clam shell. "Try bending over," she urged. "And don't breathe." His taut thigh muscle twitched as she fingered the key from the very warm bottom of his pocket, and when she looked up at him, he had the inscrutable look of a man doing long division in his head. She took a deep breath and rapidly reviewed her multiplication tables.

The shiny black door was surrounded by small glass panes; the knocker and handle were of old, polished brass that gleamed in the sun.

"It's a beautiful house," she breathed.

"My great-grandfather bought it in 1872, and my grandfather was born here two years later. My father was born here, too. He was the first artist in a long and very dull line of bankers. He's retired now; they live in Italy, so I rent out the ground floor."

As they walked down the central hall to the kitchen, Kate glanced through open doorways, noting living room, library, dining room, bedroom, bedroom, bedroom, kitchen—and fireplaces everywhere.

"Giulio, this place is enormous. How do you keep it up?"

"That's Serafina's department. I inherited her when my parents moved to Italy and I moved back in. She's actually a third cousin once removed, or something like that. She cleans, dusts, polishes, takes care of my laundry, irons my sheets, sews my shirt buttons back on, does my marketing during the week, and occasionally cooks my dinner. She's my Mrs. Wing."

"And how old is this paragon?"

"Oh . . ."—he looked at her teasingly—"sixty-plenty. She's been with my family since I was a child."

"What do you do with all this space?"

"Someday it will be filled," he pronounced. "Would you like to look around while I unpack all this stuff and make us some lunch?"

Kate retraced her steps down the long hall that ran the length of the house from front to back. She stood in the library, smiling to herself at finding it so traditional. Of course—the long line of Fraser bankers. Gilt-stamped calf bindings glinted from the mahogany shelves that covered every wall. A massive oak library table and Windsor chairs filled the center of the room. A leather couch and two club chairs faced the fireplace, and above the mantle a portrait of a kilted Fraser ancestor looked down fiercely. Though his eyes were as blue as the sky

behind him and his hair a mass of golden curls, Kate
fancied she could see something of Giulio in the intensity
of his gaze and the set of his jaw.

From the dark richness of the library she crossed the
hall to the living room opposite, and it was like stepping
into a cube of light. A pale antique Chinese carpet covered most of the pale oak floor. The walls were covered
with raw silk the color of new-mown wheat; the woodwork and ceiling were painted ivory. A wheat-colored
couch with two matching chairs and a carved Chinese
coffee table were the only furniture, and they, like the
walls, seemed to retreat into obscurity. They obviously
existed only to create a setting for the paintings.

Kate caught her breath, blinking in disbelief. She
stepped closer to the painting above the fireplace. It was
a Bonnard! It really was—a painting of the artist's wife
stepping radiant from her bath into a glowing shaft of
sunlight. Kate turned in a slow circle. There were only
two other paintings in the room: a very large Monet—
all flickering and floating light—of water hyacinths in
his garden at Giverny, and an enormous Rothko—a wall-
filling canvas stained with the mists of a garden that
never existed, a meditation on an imaginary space in a
time that never was. Kate stood transfixed with wonder.

Eagerly she pulled apart the double doors to the dining
room to discover a perfect eighteenth-century room, complete with polished mahogany table, Chippendale chairs
and highboy, and white woodwork against walls of the
palest apricot.

"Giulio," she exclaimed, returning to the kitchen, "this
is a treasure house. I never in my life expected to see
such paintings outside a museum. I'm stunned."

Giulio grinned. "My grandfather made only one trip
to Europe in his entire life; he believed holidays were a

waste of precious time and therefore sinful. Work and kirk was the family motto. He was fifty-four when he saw his first Impressionist paintings—and it was like a load of bricks falling on him. He came back from Paris with the Bonnard and the Monet. Not a bad eye for a banker."

Kate shook her head. "I still can't believe it."

"It's time for lunch. I think it's warm enough to eat in the garden, don't you? I'll carry the tray, you get the door. Up those steps," he said, indicating the stairway at the back of the hall that separated the kitchen from the bedrooms across from it.

The roof had been transformed into a summer garden, fragrant with mock orange and herbs. Tubs of flowers and ornamental trees were everywhere. Clematis and ivy climbed up white trellises, and a grape arbor completely enclosed one side. High tubs of rhododendron bloomed scarlet and orange. Low boxes of primroses ranged from deep crimson and magenta to pink and white. There were masses of white azaleas and urns of dogwood. Beside the grape arbor Giulio had planted pots of herbs and staked tomato plants.

"It's like a world apart up here," Kate murmured. "The city could be a thousand miles away."

"It takes a lot of work, but it's worth it. Let's eat." He set down his tray on a table between two chaises. "This is a real country lunch, to go with the garden."

There were sliced cucumbers and scallions dressed with olive oil and vinegar, cubes of Parmesan cheese and chunks from one of the crusty loaves, spicy olives, a plate of sliced oranges sprinkled with sugar, and a bottle of white wine.

When they had eaten everything on the tray, Kate sighed happily and leaned back in her chaise, closing her eyes. She lifted her face to the sun, luxuriating in its warmth and stretching languidly. She felt as if she were breaking out of a restraining winter shell.

What would it be like, she wondered, to live in this beautiful house, with this exuberant man? How many more contradictory currents would she discover in him? In herself? Everything he did he did with such passionate intensity—it would probably be exhausting to be around him on a daily basis . . . but how intoxicating . . . And yet there was such gentleness in him, she thought, remembering how he had sensed her grief when they were looking at the picture of Polly's grandmother and he had taken her hand.

"Are you asleep?" he whispered.

Her eyes snapped open. "No, I'm wide awake." But she must have dozed off, because he had changed into slacks and a white shirt, and the tray was gone.

He crouched beside her. "I'm so very glad you're here." He took her hand to help her up, but neither one moved. His eyes held hers in a gaze of such intensity that she could hardly breathe. Whatever vital energy sustained her life drained from her body and passed through her eyes into his. And yet in the next instant she felt the energy return, multiplied now, enhanced, increased to some power beyond number. Her hand tightened on his. With infinite gentleness, as though she were as friable as a web of spun glass, his lips touched hers in a kiss of overwhelming tenderness and longing.

He drew back a few inches and cupped her face between his hands, his dark eyes searching hers. "Oh, Kate," he whispered. "Will you be my Kate?"

"Yes, Giulio," she said, kissing his fingertips as they touched her lips. "Yes."

He held her close, burying his face in her hair. He

smelled of sandalwood and ferns. She felt his body tense against hers, hard with need, as he stretched out beside her, his mouth drinking insatiably at her lips, his tongue seeking, his lips worshipping hers.

"I want you so much, Kate," he murmured, pressing her hard against him on the narrow chaise.

"And I want...I want..." she began.

"What do you want, my Kate?"

She wasn't able to continue.

His fingers flew to the buttons of her blouse, and she buried her hands in his tumbling black hair, drawing his head to her breasts, feeling his rough curls teasing her nipples.

"Oh, Kate," he groaned, his breath seeming to tear at his throat. "I adore you!"

His hands raked her thighs, and suddenly there was no time for tender kisses and lingering caresses. His eager hands and voracious mouth ravaged her breasts, plunging her into a heedless whirlwind of desire and abandon, making her body throb beneath him. Greedily she clung to him, ravenous for his mouth, his hands, his thrusting flesh. His mouth enveloped hers, his tongue searching and probing hungrily. He pulled from her thighs their restraining sheath of pantyhose. She tore at his belt, pressing his hard, muscled hips against her. They devoured each other in an instant, their bodies consuming one another like two blazing suns, radiant with unleashed passion. They strained together to a wild fulfillment, melted into one, and lay panting in each other's arms.

"Dearest Kate," he said at last. "It wasn't supposed to happen like that."

Gently now she cradled his head between her breasts. "Soft lights and music?" She wound locks of his hair around her fingers, decking herself with rings of curls.

"Something like that." One hand cupped her breast.

Like an apple, she thought. "I didn't want to wait," she assured him. She kissed the top of his head.

"I knew that this morning," he confessed. His thumb brushed gently over her nipple.

"Did it show that much?"

"Like flags and banners, Kate. You're deliciously transparent. Your guilelessness is wildly exciting to an old roué like me."

"You're not old, darling, and I'm not so guileless as you think. Can't we have the soft lights later?"

"Hmm," he said, kissing her breast. "I promise. But now"—he sat up—"you're going to help me cook."

"Now?"

"Now!" He rearranged their disheveled clothing, kissed her soundly on the lips, helped her to her feet, and led her down the stairs.

In the kitchen he wrapped a long white apron around her. "Roll up your sleeves," he said, knotting the apron strings and kissing the back of her neck. "First we stuff the roast."

"Not before you give me a proper kiss," Kate protested, turning within the circle of his arms.

"This is the last one until after dinner," he threatened, "or we'll never eat." His lips were tender, tantalizing her with passion promised. "Now," he said, taking a step back, "this recipe has been in my mother's family for generations. This isn't *haute cuisine*, this is family cooking—no disguising sauces. Italian food enhances life, it doesn't hide it—"

"Darling, you're lecturing again. And how can we cook with your arms around me?"

"We can't," he said and sighed. He tossed some fresh rosemary leaves into a marble mortar. "You mash these while I chop the garlic." When both tasks were accomplished he made a single slice in the veal, opening it like a book.

"Now, sprinkle on your rosemary. Delicious," he said, kissing her fingertips. "I'll add the chopped garlic. Hand me that pepper mill . . . and now I roll it up and tie it . . . and I need one of your delicious fingers for the knots, please. There, and there, and there. *Ecco!* We have the beginning for arrosto di vitello. Can you say that?"

"Arrosto . . ." Kate began and faltered.

"With gusto. You must trill the *r* with the tip of your tongue. *Arrrrrrah! Arrrrrrah!* Try that."

"Arrrrrah!" she repeated dutifully. "Arrosta—"

"Arrost-o. Arrosto di vitello."

"Arrosto di vitello."

"Bene!" He kissed her quickly, the tip of his tongue flirting with hers.

"Is the cook supposed to meddle with the scullery maid?" She kissed his chin. "I thought I had to wait until after dinner."

"Ah, but that's the cook's prerogative."

Kate peeled and diced potatoes and then sat on a high stool to watch Giulio prepare his onions and brown the roast. He brought to his cooking the same passionate intensity he gave to his work, she noticed.

Together they set the table in the dining room and carried the plates and platters to the warming oven. Then they relaxed at the kitchen table, surrounded by the delicious aromas of roasting veal and simmering onions. Every few minutes Giulio got up to adjust a flame, baste the roast, stir the potatoes. He moved around the kitchen with such practiced economy of effort that Kate thought he must be the most elegant cook in the world.

He opened a chilled bottle of Grave. "We'll have this

with the first course." He turned to take the roast from
the oven, put it in the warming oven, and put a pot of
water on to boil. "Are you hungry?"

"I'm starved. Just watching you cook, among other
things, gives me an appetite."

"That's my Kate!" He gave her a smacking kiss before
turning his attention to mashing a chunk of Gorgonzola
into a pan of cream. "Now off to the dining room with
you. Light the candles; I'll be there in a minute."

Decorously Kate seated herself at the long table, set
now for only the two of them. How many generations,
she wondered, had sat here in the candlelight? Back to
his great-grandfather, that was four, she calculated.

Suddenly Giulio was beside her. He kissed the top of
her head and set a soup plate of pasta before her. "This
is fettuccine al Gorgonzola," he said, filling her wineglass and seating himself across from her. "Eat. *Man-
giara.*"

She sampled a forkful. The fresh noodles were lightly
coated with a smooth, pungent sauce of cheese and cream.

"Do you like it?" he asked anxiously.

"It's heaven. I think I could live on this. At least I'd
like to try. The cream takes the sharp edge off the cheese,
doesn't it?" She finished her serving in reverent silence
and looked up to find he had been watching her.

"You may never learn to cook like an Italian, but you
already know how to eat like one."

"And how do Italian's eat?"

"With gusto, with zest, and with love. *Con amore.*"
He rose to clear the table and put a restraining hand on
her shoulder. "Sit. I serve."

In a few moments he returned with a platter of sliced
veal, little cubes of fried potatoes, and a bowl of sweet-
sour onions. "In this house," he said, "we serve family-

style." He filled her plate and poured Médoc for them both.

"Everything's delicious," she said. "This is the most remarkable meal I've ever had, and you've given me some pretty remarkable meals lately."

He smiled happily. "It is good, isn't it? Would you like a bit more veal?"

"Oh, I couldn't."

"Have it *senza pane*," he said, putting a little from each dish on her plate and handing it back.

"What does that mean?"

"*Senza pane* means without bread. When your Italian mother says it, it means you can always eat another helping if you eat it without bread."

Kate began to feel she had been caught up in an ancient ritual, eating the food so lovingly prepared by this fiery man who spread before her the fruits of the earth. He seemed so in touch with the seasons, so attuned to the sheltering bosom of the earth, that Kate felt they could have been eating in a farmhouse.

When he had cleared their plates and brought the salad, it was almost as if he had been reading her thoughts.

"Now that my parents live in Italy," he said, "my mother's been able to put in a proper vegetable garden. That was something she dearly missed after she married my father and moved to New York. Now she can grow anything she wants for the kitchen. My father takes care of the fruit trees, and he paints, of course. He taught painting here for thirty years, at the Art Students League. The week after he retired he bought a small farmhouse with a tiny orchard from one of Mother's cousins, and two months later they were packed and away. It's very beautiful there, and there's lots of family around to keep an eye on them."

"It sounds like a dream come true."

"It is. My father was always blessed with an extraordinarily clear vision of what his life should be. And he's a very persistent man."

"As is his son, I'd say."

"He met my mother while he was on a painting holiday in Italy. Within a week he had asked her to marry him. He always insisted that he would have asked her sooner, but it took him that long to learn enough Italian to make himself understood. And he never doubted his vision of his work, either. I think he must be rather like your mother in that. Talent for him is a given. You must have the courage to allow it to take you where it will. He always says, 'You must nurture your vision as you cherish your wife.'"

"He does sound like her."

"I'd like to have a place like theirs someday," he said.

"So would I. When I get far enough ahead, I'm going to put a down payment on a little place up in Woodstock that I've had my eye on for a couple of years. But why haven't you ever bought a country retreat?"

"It's not a retreat from the world I want, not a place to hole up in and play hermit. I want a place to share, to someday nurture my family."

"I see," she said thoughtfully. "And what else would you like to do?"

"Shall I confess to you my most secret wish?"

"Yes, do."

"I'd like to be able to sing," he admitted with a laugh. "But I can't carry a tune in a bucket."

"Well, I'm not too hot on the piano, so you've got company."

"Let me get the cheese. I'm going to warm it in the oven for a second."

The Gorgonzola tasted mellow and nutty, with a tingly sharpness. They spread it with sweet French butter on crusty chunks of bread. When they had finished the last of the wine, he brought her a slice of the beautiful Nuage.

She tasted a forkful and closed her eyes, the better to savor the tartness of the brandied apples, the richness of the cream, and the crisp pastry. "This must be what angels eat."

"Now you know why the *putti,* the baby angels in Renaissance paintings, are all smiling."

"And all chubby. I don't think I can finish it."

"My dear, that's perfectly all right. You may take my word for it—the Wicked Witch of the West will not snatch you away if you don't clean your plate."

He brought a tray of coffee cups and a tiny espresso pot. "Coffee in the library in front of the fire?"

"I'll take the tray," said Kate. "You start the fire."

Soon they had settled themselves on the library couch in front of the fire, their legs stretched out beneath the coffee table. Giulio put his arm around her, and she nestled against his shoulder as they sipped their coffee and watched the dancing flames.

He kissed the top of her head. "Tell me about your dream house in the country. What's it like? Why did you choose Woodstock?"

"I have some friends there—a married couple. They have this tumbledown old farmhouse on their property. You can't see it from their place; it's on the other side of the hill. There's a little wood behind it and a meadow in front. They've been using it as an emergency guest-house, but it's going to take a lot of fixing up to make it really livable. There's a stream in the wood that widens into a little pool. And the pool's full of beautiful, but very crafty, trout."

"Don't tell me you fish," he said, nibbling her ear.

"I certainly do, sir. I also cook them, you'll be happy to learn. My father started teaching me to fly cast when I was younger than Polly. I also tie flies, of course."

"Of course." His fingers played with the curls at the back of her neck. "Would you teach me?"

"To fly fish?"

"Why not? You forget, I'm a city boy, born and bred. It's something I've always wanted to be able to do."

"Why?"

"So that someday I can teach my sons." He got up to put another log on the fire and stood for a long time gazing into the flames. When he sat down again he turned to face her, and the leaping flames were reflected in his eyes. "Will you teach me, Kate?"

"Yes, Giulio," she said, and with one finger she began to trace the outline of his cheek and mouth.

He touched her face, and it was as though they were twins, long parted, met again—mirror images verifying their likeness.

Slowly, with loving deliberation, never moving closer, he removed her blouse and brassiere. He smiled with wonder, his eyes crinkling with delight.

"You are perfection, *cara mia*, perfection." Lightly his fingers followed the contours of her shoulders; softly his hands cupped her breasts.

"Ahh," he said, smiling at her breasts in satisfaction.

Kate looked down. Her nipples stood erect, strawberry sentinels aching to be kissed. Deep within she felt a torrent of fire rising through her body. She tried to whisper his name, but the only sound that emerged was a moan.

With a slowness and deliberation equal to his, she unbuttoned his shirt. There again was that hard muscled chest, curling tufts of black hair disappearing in a V toward his belly. She caught her fingers in the coarse curls and raised her eyes to his, pleading now. But he held her away from him, his eyes half-closed, his lips parted. The fire rose within her, and his restraint was driving her to frenzy.

When at last he removed the rest of her clothes, slid quickly out of his, and drew her slowly to him, when at last she felt the hardness of his chest against her yielding breasts, then the heat of his body met the raging fire within her, arousing in her a passion greater than she had ever known before. She locked her hands behind his neck, and when his mouth covered hers, she sucked his tongue into her mouth. She ached to possess him and to be possessed utterly.

Wherever his mouth went, there her spirit followed as her desire rushed to answer his kisses. He traced the curve of her neck with his lips and set a trail of fire across her throat. When he drew each nipple in turn into his hot mouth, she cried out in pleasure. She lay in his arms while he caressed her body as though creating, forming, shaping it from its primordial clay. He buried kisses in her belly while his urgent hands brought fire to her thighs. He kissed the backs of her knees, and she began to tremble as a leaping flame of desire rose, darting, rising higher, never quenched. When she knew she could bear it no longer, she called his name over and over, pleading until he took her in his arms again.

Kate surrendered to him as though taken by a sea god beneath the sea, her limbs borne down by the weight of waves it was beyond her power to resist. Seawater filled her eyes, roared rushing into her ears, pouring into every cranny of her body, bearing her swiftly deeper, ever deeper into a blackness of heaving currents. Brilliant streams of phosphorescence exploded behind her eyelids.

Slowly, slowly . . . she rose toward the surface, drift-
ing at the center of a tidepool where shallow waters
lapped languidly against her and exquisite anemones
trailed from her fingers' end. She lay suspended, transformed forever into a creature of the teeming, life-giving
sea, subject to the moon, to tides, to the magnificent sea
god who, in taking her, carrying her on this journey
beneath the sea, had changed her forever.

"I love you," she whispered.

"I love you, *cara mia*," he murmured in reply. He
rose from the couch to stand above her, his body bronzed
by the dying flames. As her gaze traveled over his body
she shivered suddenly, remembering both his power and
his gentleness.

Stooping, he gathered her easily into his arms and
carried her to the bedroom. She licked his throat; he
tasted like the sea.

His kisses now were more urgent, his hands bolder.
Their bodies locked again in the elemental motion of the
sea; he plunged her once more far beneath the pulsing
waves, thrusting her into unexplored caverns agleam with
coral and mother of pearl.

Slowly, once again, she rose to float in her tidepool.

"I love you . . . I love you," he breathed softly, and
then she sank into oblivion.

CHAPTER NINE

KATE STRETCHED LUXURIOUSLY. She felt drugged, her limbs languid. Reaching with her toes for the bottom of the bed, she arched her back and crooked her arm over her eyes to block the sunlight. She smiled secretly to herself; her arm smelled of Giulio and the sea.

"Good morning, darling," Giulio whispered, taking her arm away. He kissed her eyelids. "I've brought you breakfast." He kissed her tenderly, his mouth sweet with honey.

Kate sat up, clutching the sheet around her. Giulio stood naked beside the bed, smiling. He set the breakfast tray on her lap and sat beside her.

"Drink your orange juice like a good girl," he commanded. "Then you may have toast and butter and honey." He poured coffee and hot milk into two mugs. "And I've brought in the morning paper. We'll have breakfast and do the crossword together and then—"

"I can't, darling," Kate said.

Lightly he stroked her cheek. "If we spend the day here, we can picnic in the garden..."

"I can't stay. I have an assignment to finish by tomorrow morning."

"Or we could go to the new Italian movie at the Little Carnegie and have a Mexican dinner uptown."

"You know I'd like to, but my deadline's tomorrow morning, and I've never missed a deadline in my life. Not once."

"On the other hand, we might go sailing. Would you like to go sailing? I know a guy who's always looking for a crew."

"I don't know how I'm going to get it all done as it is."

"No, I don't want to share you with someone else. How would you like an old-fashioned, romantic carriage ride through Central Park?"

"And I have a nagging feeling I'm low on illustration board. It would be just my luck to run out before—"

"Stay with me," he whispered, stroking her thigh through the sheet.

"Darling, what are you doing?"

"Tantalizing you...Think of the pleasures in store for you if we spend the day together."

"It's not that I don't want to," she said, laughing and grabbing his ears, pulling his mouth to hers for a long, satisfying breakfast kiss. The sheet fell from her, and he began kissing her breasts.

"Giulio," she protested, "you'll spill the coffee. Don't you want me to be successful? And sought after by every art director in town?"

"Only from nine to five and never on weekends," he growled, slipping into bed beside her and snuggling her against him. He put his arm around her so that he could cup her breast in one hand and hold his coffee in the other. He sighed contentedly. "Now, tell me how you want to spend the day, my love." He squeezed her breast playfully. "Aren't you my love today?"

"I'm yours every day—after today. Tomorrow I'll be yours. Once this job is out of the way, we'll make up for missing today." She kissed him lightly. "I promise."

His hand on her breast was not so playful now; his lips turned hard and demanding. "Why not now?"

"Because I must work, my love. Truly. Deadlines are deadlines."

"Nonsense. Art directors' deadlines are always fictitious."

"They may be to you, but not to me. Can't we have dinner tomorrow?"

"I can't tomorrow."

"There, you see—what's sauce for the goose—"

"That means I'll only see you in the office tomorrow."

"What time is it anyway?"

"Noon."

"Oh, no! Hand me a robe or something."

"A robe? Why do you want a robe?"

"Midwestern modesty, darling. It comes over me with the dawn. Please."

Chuckling at her, Giulio brought her his shower robe. It nearly covered her feet. "You'll find extra toothbrushes in the medicine cabinet," he called after her as she closed the bathroom door.

Kate opened the cabinet to find a neat stack of packaged toothbrushes. And what, she asked herself, are the implications of *five* toothbrushes? She didn't even want to think about it. She had just finished brushing her teeth when she heard Giulio's knock at the door.

"May I come in?"

"Yes," she said, puzzled.

"Have you showered?"

"No, I've just brushed my teeth."

"Splendid!" he said, grabbing her hand and leading her toward the shower.

"Don't be foolish," she protested. "There's not enough room in there for the two of us."

"There is if we stand close enough," he said, taking a firm grip on her arm. "Hot or medium?" He turned on the taps.

"Hot, very hot," she said, grinning now. "Oh, Giulio, I feel so silly."

"Nonsense, my girl, how else can you be sure your back is really clean? In you go."

Kate stepped laughing into the shower and let the spray run over her while Giulio busily lathered her everywhere as meticulously and vigorously as he might a grubby child.

Grinning, Kate said, "I haven't taken a shower with anyone since sixth-grade gym class, and believe me, Cookie Keeler was nothing like you."

"Rinse," he said, turning her in a circle under the spray. "Hey! You've splashed soap in my eyes," he wailed.

"Here," she said, handing him a washcloth. "Wipe it out with this."

"Oh, God, it stings!"

"Stop rubbing, you'll only make it worse. You're such a baby," she crooned, putting her arms around him and kissing each eye in turn.

He held her tightly as the water poured over them, his kisses growing hungrier and more urgent as he pressed against her, his morning beard scratching her throat.

"Darling," she moaned, "not here."

"Why not?" he said with a laugh, water streaming down his face.

"For one thing, we'll fall."

"Nonsense, my toes grip like a lemur's," he said, locking his forearms beneath her and lifting her to him.

"Put me down, you idiot."

"Are you my Kate?" he demanded. "Mine?"

"Yes, Giulio," she whispered, surprised by the hint of anger in his voice.

"Then stop struggling," he commanded, covering her mouth with his.

Kate toweled herself dry and left Giulio to his shaving. She returned to the bedroom to find the bed made and her clothes carefully laid out. She smiled to herself. I'm in love with a very tactful man. Possessive and demanding, but tactful.

She walked through room after room, calling his name until she saw the garden door open at the top of the hall stairs. He had pulled on a pair of cut-off jeans and was pruning a tubbed orange tree. Kate slipped up behind him and, wrapping her arms around his chest, rested her cheek against his bare back.

He turned to hold her. "Kate, you can't leave like this. We have so much to talk about."

"Yes, I know, but not today. I really must work. And I need some time to think. I honestly don't believe I can think clearly when I'm with you; not today, at least."

"You should let your body think for you. I think you spent your whole life denying your body before yesterday. Am I right?"

She searched his black eyes for a hint of mockery but found none. Dare she admit to him how completely, how devastatingly, he had changed her life, obliterated her past? She stood pressed against him, knowing he had created her anew: she was Aphrodite, born of the sea. For the moment she wanted nothing but to be with him. The sun, shining on this newborn present with Giulio, dazzled her eyes, and she could not see into the future.

"Am I right? Tell me," he insisted.

She could not speak, fearing to admit how vulnerable she felt, as fragile as any other newborn creature.

"Kate?"

"Yes, Giulio. You're right."

"Then stay with me." His arms locked her to him so tightly she could hardly breathe. "Just a little longer." His mouth ravaged hers, rekindling the fires that lay so lightly banked.

"I can't stay, darling. You know I want to, but I can't. Please let me go."

"You shouldn't be working nights and weekends." His hands molded her body to his. "You should be in my arms." He buried kisses in her neck, and her knees turned to water.

"Please," she gasped. "Let me go."

Suddenly he released her. "Tonight?"

"Tomorrow," she insisted.

Once she returned to her apartment, Kate kept doggedly at her work throughout the long afternoon. Her hands moved automatically while her mind raced, thinking of nothing but Giulio. What had she gotten herself into, she asked herself. She'd broken all her own rules. She'd fallen in love with the man she worked for—mistake number one. At least people were always saying it was asking for trouble to get involved with your employer. Well, just because everyone said it was a big mistake didn't mean she couldn't make it work. So to hell with rule number one. Mistake number two: he was already involved with Liz. She had to work with that woman, which could make life a living misery. And Giulio could short-circuit her better judgment with a single kiss, and she'd let him know it—mistake number three.

How could she have spent all day yesterday with him—and all night and half of today—and never once thought about Liz, she wondered. How could she have let her emotions cloud her good sense like that? He couldn't really be serious about her and involved with Liz at the same time. She must have been doing an awful lot of wishful thinking last night.

Kate felt like a watch too tightly wound, her gears jammed against Giulio's demanding vitality. All the things that had seemed to give her life shape before she met him now seemed limiting, the boundaries cold. She longed for his warming passion. In his arms she felt the very contours of her life thawing, melting into formlessness. What would she be left with? Would she be able to withstand his intensity, or would she be absorbed into his personality, losing all sense of herself?

He made her feel so vital, so alive, that in merely walking beside him her step felt lighter and a great bubble of life rose in her chest, knocking against the back of her throat, ready to explode . . . Perhaps she would shed her old, hermetic existence . . . perhaps with a bit of his vitality glowing inside her, she would make a new life. She felt that this buoyancy within her could sustain her to meet anything, do anything.

"Oh, damn!" she said aloud. No matter how wonderful he made her feel, Kate knew he wasn't hers. He was someone else's, so there was no point in worrying about how to keep herself from being swallowed up by him.

Tomorrow. She'd see him tomorrow. But what would she say? She was to meet with Jeffrey and Liz at two. How could she look Liz in the eye? And what would Liz say? Would she guess something was up?

Too restless now to work, Kate pulled on a jacket, determined to walk until the exercise calmed her down and cleared her head. She headed for the park, hoping its early-summer greenness would refresh her spirits. But everyone she saw appeared to be paired. Couples walking hand in hand filled every path; couples lay tanning together in the sun; families picnicked in the meadows; even the joggers were running in pairs. She had never felt so alone. After an hour she returned to her work more miserable than ever.

She made herself a cheese sandwich and ate it standing at her kitchen counter, washing it down with a glass of milk. It tasted like sawdust. How she loved Giulio's passion for food—his eyes shining with the light of the convinced preaching to the heathen as he tried to make her a convert to tastes that might have been commonplace to him but that were exotic to her. And his loving insistence that she taste this, sample that . . . She loved him for caring so much, peering into the leafy depths of a sheaf of Romaine or scrutinizing a cheese with the same intensity she saw in his eyes when he studied a drawing or a photograph.

Even if she ignored the fact that she worked for him, she thought, she didn't know how she could even think of making a commitment to a man who was involved with someone else. Because she wanted him! That was why, she grimly acknowledged. He'd just have to uninvolve himself . . . He might think it old-fashioned, but he was going to have to choose between her and Liz. Either way, her working relationship with Liz was probably going to be impossible. But she was determined that this wouldn't be one of those casual affairs that was over before it was properly started. Not if she could help it. Liz might have known him longer, but . . .

She reached for the phone and dialed Marion's number. As soon as she heard her friend's comforting voice she felt her own choke up. She swallowed hard.

"Marion, can you come over for an early supper tomorrow?"

"Kate, what's wrong?"

"N–nothing's wrong. I just need to talk."

"Listen, I have this huge casserole I made last night, and there's tons left. I'll bring it over. You make the salad. Are you sure you're all right?"

"I'm not sure about anything just now, except that tomorrow I'm going to have to start fighting for someone I love and I'm not sure how to begin."

"Someone you love? Kate! Not that twerp Neal!" Marion had never thought Kate and Neal were a good match.

"No, don't be silly. It's Giulio Fraser."

"Fraser, your art director? Boy, he works fast. If you love him, what are you fighting for?"

"He's involved with someone else."

"Oops! That means nothing but trouble. Are you sure you don't want me to come over now? You don't sound all that good."

"I guess I'm not, but tomorrow's soon enough. I'll be okay."

"Try to get some sleep. Don't sit up half the night worrying over this thing. Promise?"

"Promise."

But her sleep was troubled by memories and confusing dreams of the sea.

CHAPTER TEN

KATE STOOD AT her living room window, sipping her morning coffee and comparing it to Giulio's. It tasted insipid. Dark clouds massed in the northern sky, promising rain. This was going to be a miserable day, she told herself. She wished she had something other than toast with onion-flavored butter. Croissants would be nice, or muffins. Grimly she ate her toast and began going over the work she had completed last night, giving it a final check before calling the messenger service for a pickup. Just as she reached for the phone, it rang.

"Hello, darling," said Giulio. "Are you having onion-toast and tea?" He didn't wait for an answer. "Did you finish your work yesterday? I called you, but you were out and you forgot to turn on your machine so I couldn't leave a message. Are you still coming in today to see Jeffrey and Liz?"

"Yes, at two."

"Good, I'll see you after." He hung up.

Furious with herself, Kate realized she had said exactly three words. He hadn't said "I love you," but then neither had she. And who did he think he was, anyway, calling her up and making fun of her breakfast? Even if it was a lousy breakfast. There was a soft clicking against her window. The rain had begun. Kate called the messenger service and ate a pot of strawberry yogurt, not because she was hungry but because she was angry, though she wasn't entirely sure why. She stood at the window waiting for the messenger and watching the rain.

The lobby intercom buzzed, and a crackly voice announced her messenger. She checked again to be certain the package was securely wrapped against the rain.

"It's a lousy day," the messenger commented when he arrived to stand wetly in her tiny hall. "Sign here." He tucked her package into his big blue carrying case and extracted another one, which he handed to her.

It smelled delicious. Kate sniffed again. It smelled like corned beef and sauerkraut.

The messenger grinned. "Everybody in Manhattan ordered Reubens for lunch Friday, and my bag still smells like a sandwich."

"Would you bring me a Reuben? From the Carnegie Deli?"

"Now? Lady, it's nine o'clock in the morning."

"Yes, now." Suddenly she was starving.

"Anything you say."

The savory package was from Angela. She had sent an approval of the Amsterdam picture, along with the review blurbs for the back cover and the copy for the jacket flap. Kate set to work specifying type, and when the messenger returned with her sandwich, she ate every last bit of it and felt immensely cheered.

By noon the sky had grown even darker. The wind sent sheets of rain lashing against her windows. She looked across at the Actress's window. Her lights were on. She was up, but this was not a day to put out crumbs. Kate wondered if she ever got involved with the actors she worked with. No, she was probably much too sensible for that.

As she pulled on her raincoat and searched the back of her closet for her umbrella, she tried to rehearse what she would say to Giulio, but she couldn't find any words. She couldn't find the umbrella, either. She grabbed a rain hat and left.

It was still pouring, and there were no empty cabs. After ten sodden minutes of waving she finally managed to stop one, but not before it had splashed her to the knees. She got in gratefully nonetheless.

"Listen, lady," said the driver. "You shouldn't be standing in the street like that. You mighta been hit. Just this morning I saw this dumb guy get his leg broke trying to get a cab."

"The cab hit him?"

"Naw, he was hit by a bus."

"Just drive," she said.

Jeffrey had cleared two long tables and arranged neat stacks of all the pictures they had taken of Gunilla. Liz was not to be seen, and Giulio's office door was closed.

"I don't know what's happened to Liz," said Jeffrey. "She hasn't come in yet. That must have been some weekend in the Hamptons."

Kate leafed through a pile of photos.

"What do you think? Will they do to draw from?" he asked.

"They'd do for full illustrations themselves," said Kate. "They're gorgeous."

"Hi!" called Liz from the doorway. "Sorry I'm late."

"I was beginning to wonder," chided Jeffrey.

"Not so loud, Jeff, darling. Mommy's hung."

Kate braced for the storm.

Jeffrey said, "You had a lovely weekend, I take it."

Liz's smile was seraphic. "Divine!" she breathed. "And you, Kate, did you have a divine weekend, too?"

"It was very nice, thank you." Kate was flummoxed. Liz was not cold or brittle or taunting. She wasn't being ironic, Kate was sure. In fact, she was friendlier than ever. She obviously had no idea how Kate had spent her weekend. Well, thought Kate, she'll find out soon enough, but not from me.

Liz opened her illustration log, and the three of them began coding the photos as Kate chose her working prints. When the job was done Liz took the photos away to be copied and Jeffrey said, "We'll send them over to you when we've finished, Kate. You've really got a big job ahead of you."

"Meeting over?" Giulio asked as he came out of his office.

Kate had been steeling herself to talk to him in his office, but he had his coat on.

"Time for tea, Kate. Get your coat."

She huddled in the building's entrance while Giulio flagged a cab. As soon as he had given the address to the driver, he took her in his arms; she shuddered at the thought of what she had to tell him.

"Darling, you're cold," he said. "We'll be there in a

minute. Did you take time for lunch today?"

"I ate it very early."

"Then an old-fashioned English tea is just what you need."

Kate spotted the little East Side tearoom when they were still half a block away. It looked like a beckoning haven, its chintz-curtained windows glowing warmly in the dark, rainy afternoon.

It was a crowded, happy room. A silver-framed picture of the Queen smiled benignly from the wall behind the cash register. The plate rail was proudly filled with Spode, Crown Derby, and Royal Worcester. Every table held a tiny Staffordshire vase of fresh flowers.

Giulio ordered two plates of sandwiches—cucumber for Kate, Gentleman's Relish on toast for himself—and scones with strawberry jam and two slices of walnut cake and tea.

"Is this another of your secret places?" Kate quizzed.

"Yes." His eyes held hers in a gaze so strong she couldn't look away. He reached across the tiny table to take her hand. "I missed you last night, my Kate."

She thought she might drown in his eyes. His hair was all tangled from the wind, and the rain still glistened in his curls. She closed her eyes and took a deep breath.

"What about Liz?" she said.

He looked puzzled. "What about her? What has Liz got to do with us?"

"But aren't the two of you...isn't she...?" Kate couldn't bring herself to put it into words. She looked down at her plate, searching desperately for another way to begin.

When she looked up, Giulio was frowning. He sat silent and unmoving. When at last he spoke, his voice was so low Kate could hardly hear him.

"Are we lovers? Is that what you're trying to say?"

She nodded.

"The answer is no, Kate."

"But I thought—that day you took us all to lunch I thought—"

"That we'd been away for the weekend together. We were. We have several friends in common. We often go to the same house parties. I want to be completely honest with you; Liz and I were lovers once, but that's hardly a secret to anyone who knows us both. Besides, that was over years ago. We parted friends, and we've stayed friends."

Tears of relief stung her eyes. She blinked them away.

"Darling," he said, his voice deep with concern, "what's wrong now?"

Waves of relief washed over her. Suddenly she felt light and filled with joy. "Giulio, I've been such an idiot. I've spent the last twenty-four hours steeling myself for an old-fashioned fight—"

"Over 'the other woman'?"

"Mainly."

"Don't you understand that I love you? You are the most enchanting and refreshing woman I have ever known."

"And probably the most foolish."

"That too," he teased. "I did a lot of thinking yesterday, while you were brooding over Liz. I was thinking about us. I don't want to see you only when you can conveniently fit me into your busy schedule. That's not enough. Do you agree?"

"Yes, darling," she said, wondering how much of a commitment he was really prepared to make.

"Good. Then the only solution is for you to move into my place."

"Move in?"

"Yes. We should be living together. I don't want to live away from you. I want to wake up every morning and find you beside me."

"But where would I work?"

"That's no problem. The small bedroom faces north; we can clear that out and you can turn it into a studio."

Kate felt panic overcome her. This was a kind of commitment she could not imagine herself making. Live together?

"Or," he continued, "you could keep your apartment uptown, if that would make you feel more secure or whatever, and just use it as your studio. But I think it would be better if—"

"But I can't give up everything, just like that."

"Why not? What are you giving up? A dinky apartment with a lousy kitchen that's not big enough to swing an omelet pan in."

"Don't you see—if I gave it up I'd feel I was living on your sufferance."

"Kate, I want to be with you as much as twenty-four hours a day permit. If you worked at my place—our place—there wouldn't have to be a lot of rushing back and forth."

"I don't think that would necessarily eliminate conflicts."

"Then we really must reorganize your work schedule so that you don't have to work in the evenings."

"Except on the nights *you* worked, when it wouldn't matter," she shot back. "Don't you see? *That's* what I mean by conflicts. Giulio, darling, I *like* working in the evenings. Besides, if I didn't, I couldn't find the time during the day to visit my accounts or go to galleries or draw in the park. Why is it necessary that my work schedule conform to yours? Why can't yours be adapted to mine? Or maybe each scrunched a little bit and we meet in the middle?"

"Look, don't get me wrong. I don't want to interfere with your work; I simply want us to be together as much as possible. Does that sound selfish?"

"It sounds like my ex-husband. It's bondage disguised as devotion."

"That's a disgusting thing to say, and I resent it. Is that how you see us? This whole discussion is beginning to sound like an old Barbara Stanwyck movie. Is my face suitably dark with wrath? I think my next line is 'Don't do this to us.'" He reached across the table to take her hand, and when she looked up she saw how much genuine anger lay beneath his flippancy.

"I don't enjoy being ridiculed," she said through clenched teeth. She stared out the window, unable to look at him now. Rain lashed at the curtained panes. Traffic clogged the street. She could hear the clink of china, the murmur of voices behind her, the high piping voice of the proprietress. She heard her thoughts saying she loved him, and that everything was in shambles. And then she heard Giulio's voice, gentle now, careful.

"Have you lived with anyone since your divorce?"

"No," she whispered, barely able to speak for the weight of sorrow she felt.

"Do you really love me, Kate?"

"Yes, you know I do."

"Then I think it's time you grew up and stopped acting like a B-movie spinster."

She turned to him, her face flushed with a fury so hot she could feel sweat prickle on her back. "And I think it's time you stopped patronizing me!"

She snatched up her coat and ran to the door. Tears

of anger mixed with the rain on her cheeks as she dashed up the street. She ran four blocks before she realized she had forgotten to button her coat. Her hat was clutched in her hand. She was soaked through. Water streamed down her face and neck, cooling her anger and seeping beneath her collar. By the time she reached Fifty-seventh Street, her shoes were soaked through, and there were no cabs in sight.

Kate squelched onto a crosstown bus. As they neared Sixth Avenue, the woman beside her got up to leave.

She touched Kate's arm. "You look like you need help," she said, handing Kate a folded slip of paper. Then the rear door opened, and the woman was gone.

Kate looked at the flier. It was headed: "Spiritual Reader. Mrs. Rosa. Palm and Card Readings. Will Help on All Problems." Not on this one, Kate thought. Beneath an execrable drawing of an open palm were the words: "I specialize on love and breaking-up problems. Also illness, health, business, and enemies." Mrs. Rosa's address and business telephone number followed. Kate wondered why her flier didn't say anything about seeing into the future. Maybe, thought Kate, it's just as dark to her as it is to me right now.

She stopped to buy salad greens and sloshed down Ninth Avenue, wondering for the hundredth time where the bag lady who usually directed traffic at her corner went when it rained. Maybe she'd gone to visit Mrs. Rosa.

Once she got home there was just time to strip off her wet clothes and take a hot shower before Marion arrived, but the shower didn't warm her. She felt chilled to her very soul.

Marion breezed in, cradling her casserole in her arms.

"Here," she said, handing it to Kate. "Put it in the oven at three twenty-five."

It was so heavy Kate thought it could easily be biblically divided to feed the multitude.

"This is putrid weather for sopranos," Marion said, unwinding the heavy muffler that protected her throat. Though her days were spent as an executive's assistant, her evenings and weekends were devoted to singing: voice lessons, chorus rehearsals, choir practice. "You look terrible," she said when the last of the scarf was unwound. "What's happened?"

"I feel terrible. Do you want a drink?"

"Of course I want a drink; a little something would be good for the throat. And you look like you need one."

"It'll have to be Scotch; I forgot to buy wine."

When they had settled on the couch with their drinks, Marion said, "Now tell me what's been going on. Start from the beginning."

"The beginning is that I've broken the working woman's first rule: I've fallen in love with someone I work for."

"Fraser."

Kate nodded.

"That's not the end of the world. Tell me about it. What's he really like? How old is he?"

"About forty, I think. He's dark—did I tell you his mother's Italian? He's unbelievably good-looking, but he's terribly..." Kate paused, searching for the right word. "Mercurial. One moment he's warm and loving and gentle, and the next moment he's patronizing, opinionated, and frighteningly possessive."

"You seem to know him pretty well. I thought you just met the guy a couple of weeks ago."

"Well, I guess I did. But we've spent a lot of time

together, and then he made dinner for me Saturday night
and—"

"He cooks, too? He sounds like a dream. So you had
dinner and what?"

"I stayed over."

"And now you regret it."

"No, as a matter of fact I don't. I love him. He says
he loves me, and I believe him."

"But yesterday you said—"

"I thought he was having an affair with someone else.
Now I know I was wrong; he's not."

"So what's the problem?"

"Marion, he wants me to move in with him."

"That's a big want. Are you ready for that?"

"I just don't know." Kate walked to the window. The
rain had stopped. The Actress's cat sat in his window,
washing his face. "We had a terrible fight this afternoon.
I know that I want him more than anything in the world,
but at the same time I want my own life, too. I'm afraid
he'll smother me. He's already talking about rearranging
my life to suit his convenience."

"You can't have a relationship without compromise.
You know that as well as I do."

"Of course I do, but suddenly this afternoon he started
sounding like my ex-husband. I don't want to go through
life as Fraser's woman. I have to be my own woman. I
fought that battle with Jack; I'm not going to fight it
again with Giulio—or barter my independence. Does
that make sense? Do you think I'm expecting too much?"

"Yes it does, and no you're not. And I need another
drink, and so do you. Let me get it."

When Marion returned with their refills, she launched
into the discussion anew. "I realize your days have been
flying on wings of love and all that, but has he had time

to mention marriage?"

"Oh, no. He jokes about himself as an old roué, which is perfectly silly, of course." She smiled to herself. "It's all part of his fantasy life. But for both of us living together would be a kind of trial, I suppose. And to tell the truth, I'd want to be absolutely certain before..." She glanced over at the cat again. It was asleep.

The oven timer pinged, and Marion said, "Let's eat before we both get drunk."

Together they made a salad and served themselves from the steaming dish.

"It's good," said Kate. It reminded her of one of her mother's Monday night dishes. She hated to think what Giulio would say if he could taste it.

"It's even better tonight than it was last night. I threw in everything I could find in the fridge."

"Last week," said Kate, "I met two photographers and their children. They've managed to work out an accommodation for their two careers—they're both very successful—and still raise two bright and loving children."

"Do you mind telling me how they fit the kids and running a household around two full-time jobs? They should write a book; they'd make a fortune."

"Their secret weapon is Mrs. Wing—full-time nanny, housekeeper, and cook. And what's wrong with a housekeeper, I ask myself. Unless you bring your kids into the office or stick them in day care, what alternative do you have?"

"I don't know. They're lucky they're successful enough to be able to afford their Mrs. Wing.

"And without Mrs. Wing, they couldn't have been successful. It's a vicious circle, isn't it?"

Marion looked at her sharply. "Kate, what are we doing talking about Mrs. Wing all of a sudden, and somebody's arrangements for their kids?"

Kate twisted the napkin in her lap. "Rick and Polly made me realize how much I wanted kids . . . someday." she blurted. "Giulio's their godfather, and they absolutely adore him."

Marion laughed. "Don't tell me—I already know. You're thinking what a wonderful father he'd make. Kate, aren't you jumping the gun?"

"I know it sounds dumb. And we had such an awful fight this afternoon. I wish I could see into the future. What I'm afraid of, I guess, is . . . Well, suppose I do move in with Giulio, and we live together happily, putting off having kids because we're not married, and then, after five years, it's over. Then where am I? Thirty-five and back to square one. You've got to admit that thirty-five is not exactly a great age to be looking for a husband or deciding to have children."

"Well, you wouldn't be a decrepit wreck, you know. Let's face it, there is no 'good age' for finding a man. Most of us have reached the age where the good ones are all married. And when those same good ones start getting divorced, they run out looking for girls in their late teens and early twenties. That's Marion's law: you're always the wrong age, no matter what it is."

"I guess you're right."

"Look, what if you married him tomorrow, had children, and in five years your marriage fell apart? Then what?"

Kate felt stricken at the thought.

"Be realistic, Kate; it happens. There's no guarantee just because you've exchanged vows."

"How well I know."

"So take the chance. Move in, see if it will work. Try your damnedest to make it work. From what you've told me about him, he probably wants children every bit as much as you do. He's Italian, isn't he?"

"Half. He asked me if I'd teach him to fly fish so that he could teach his sons."

"Well, there you are! There aren't many men around like your Giulio. Grab him while you can!"

For a long time after Marion left, Kate sat staring at the phone, trying to make up her mind to call Giulio. She finally decided she was going to have to be strong enough not to allow herself to be dominated. That was all there was to it. She wanted him, but not at the expense of her own life. If he loved her as much as he said he did, there had to be a way to work things out.

She picked up the receiver and realized she didn't know his telephone number. She hauled the big Manhattan directory up from beneath her drawing table. The Frasers ran from Alice to William. No Ian was listed and no Giuliano. None lived on Eleventh Street. She should have guessed he'd be unlisted. She'd have to wait and call him at his office in the morning.

She put the directory back beneath the table and turned to look at the night sky. It glowed pink and gold, reflecting the lights of the city. On the sidewalk below a few dogs were being given their late-night exercise.

Then she saw Giulio. He stood beneath the streetlight, looking up, scanning the building, seemingly counting the floors, looking for her apartment.

"Here, darling. Here I am," she whispered.

At last he spotted her and began a tentative wave. She beckoned silently to him: Come up, oh, please come up!

For a long moment he stood there, his hands once more plunged deep into his raincoat pockets, the wind blowing his hair. Then suddenly he was running toward the lobby.

CHAPTER ELEVEN

KATE WAS THE first to find her voice. Giulio held her so close she found herself speaking into the lapels of his coat. "Can you forgive me for being such an idiot?"

Giulio hugged her even tighter. "If you'll forgive me for being such a pompous ass."

"We really must talk."

One black eyebrow shot up in a mocking arc. "Perhaps we'd better not. We seem to do so much better when we don't talk." The corners of his mouth curved mischievously.

"Be serious, darling, and give me your coat."

"Yes, dear," he said, all mock submissiveness as he allowed Kate to lead him to the couch.

"Giulio, why are you wearing a tux?"

"Because we're going to a party."

Before she could say another word, he took her in his arms. His mouth was insistent, his tongue greedy, as though they had been parted not for a few hours but for years. He kissed her hungrily, like a distant voyager home from the sea. Then he held her slightly away from himself, looking into her eyes.

"Do you want a drink?" she finally asked.

"No, I want you. Come here; I have something to say." He took her hand, led her over to the couch, and pulled her down onto his lap. "Now this is what I call cozy," he said, cuddling her against him. "Kate, I was wrong this afternoon, insisting the way I did that you move in. I was rushing you. I'm afraid I've developed a very bad case of middle-aged eagerness."

"You're not middle-aged."

"Then let's say I've become very conscious lately of how quickly time is passing. I want to live with you—"

"But I—"

"Hush," he said, laying a finger against her lips. "Let me finish. It doesn't matter if you're not ready to move in with me now. I'm willing to wait for you to come to the decision in your own time. Will you think about it?"

"Since this afternoon I've thought about nothing else. I'd like to wait, Giulio, until we know each other better. We don't really know each other that well."

His lips brushed the corners of her mouth. "I wouldn't say that."

"You know what I mean."

He kissed the tip of her nose. "At least you know I'm not seeing another woman."

"Indeed I do. Tell me something..."

"Hmm?" He nibbled on her earlobe.

"What were you doing with all those extra tooth-brushes?"

Laughter burst from him in a joyous rumble. "They

were on sale at McKay's—six for six fifty—you jealous ninny." He hugged her closer. "After you blazed out on me this afternoon, our waitress handed me the bill and said, 'You must have been beastly to send that sweet girl away in tears. You go after her and tell her you're sorry.'"

"What did you say?"

"I didn't say anything. I felt pretty foolish. Then she slammed my change down on the table and said, 'You lads are all alike!'"

"Poor darling. And I thought the English were so reticent. We mustn't ever fight like that again. I was so miserable afterward."

"Where did you go? I didn't see you anywhere when I got out onto the street."

"I stalked down Madison Avenue until I'd cooled off, and then I came home. My friend Marion brought a casserole over, and the two of us had dinner and talked. I've been thinking a lot about Melissa and Simon."

"What was in the casserole?"

"If they could work out all the problems they had to face, I don't see why we can't."

"What was in the casserole?"

"Oh, uh, all kinds of things—celery, onions, broccoli, some Brussels sprouts, I think, green peppers, carrots, peas, lots of noodles, a couple of cans of mushroom soup, and potato chips on top."

He shuddered. "It sounds ghastly."

"I knew you'd say that."

"I'm sorry, that was rude. I'm sure it was delicious."

"It was kind of gluey, actually," she admitted, feeling like a traitor.

"Ha! I'm converting you."

"I'm still a little wary, but I think you are."

"Are you too wary to have dinner with me tomorrow night?"

"Not if you're cooking."

"Now how would you like to go to a party?"

"Tonight? But it's after ten, and I have a lot of work tomorrow. Do you have to go? Can't we stay here?" She ran her fingers through his wind-tangled hair and pulled at his tie.

"I have to go," he said, grabbing her hands and holding them against his chest. "Do you know Don Ricci, the stage designer? We went to school together. His play opened at the Booth tonight, and I promised I'd show up at Sardi's for the company party."

"Oh, Giulio, how marvelous! I've never been to an opening night party. What should I wear?"

"You can wear anything you want to an opening night party—it doesn't matter."

"Then why are you wearing black tie?" Kate shook her head. "You lads are all alike. Make yourself a drink," she called as she raced to her bedroom. "I'll be ready in thirty minutes."

Kate's best dress was neither black nor basic but jade-green silk jersey, chosen to match her eyes. It was cut very high in the front and was completely bare in the back, with an open V that stopped just below her waist. She hung pearl drops from her ears and sprayed herself liberally with her most expensive perfume. Her evening coat was of matching taffeta, high-collared and lined with blue-green Japanese silk.

Giulio stood up the moment he caught sight of her. She carried her evening coat to him and turned in a slow circle before him.

"Kate . . . oh, Kate," he said on a long, slow breath, his eyes glowing with pleasure. "Let's forget the party."

He dropped her coat onto the couch and moved closer. His hands smoothed over her silken hips. "Let's stay here."

"Not on your life," she laughed, whirling out of his reach. "I wouldn't miss this for the world."

Giulio gave his name at the press table and carried Kate's coat to the checkroom. "The Belasco Room is beyond the bar," he said, gesturing to his left toward a very small space packed with a great many people. "I'll run interference—give me your hand."

As they wormed their way through the crush, she nearly bumped into a startlingly familiar woman with deep violet eyes and enough diamonds to light up all of Broadway. She was laughing raucously at something the man beside her had just said. His eyes crinkled with laughter behind horn-rimmed glasses, and his smile was big enough to encompass all the earth.

"Giulio," she whispered when they had wedged around the couple, "wasn't that—?"

"Yes," he said, "it was."

They turned into a small cocktail area, but there they were blocked by a tight knot of people. A woman with the speckled gray curls of a silver poodle was saying to a cherubic blond man, "I was just talking to Jean."

"Don't tell me; I know. She hated it," he said.

"She said that compared to the London production, it was mingy."

"I don't want to hear about it. I cried through the whole second act. Do you suppose there's any food left?" His voice was plaintive. "Why is the food always gone by the time the actors get here?"

Giulio tightened his grip on Kate's hand and pulled

her through into a beautiful room, darkly paneled from
floor to ceiling and crowded with the play's company
and their friends. Some sat at tables, others stood in small
groups, and many waited at the long buffet. Giulio was
right. They wore everything from the most elegant evening clothes to jeans and turtlenecks. One young woman,
who appeared to be clothed entirely in shawls, stood on
tiptoe with her head bent back, listening raptly to an
amazingly tall, very skinny young man in a white suit.

Kate had expected to see a lot of worried-looking,
haggard actors waiting nervously for the impending reviews, but everyone was laughing and chatting with care-
free delight. That, she said to herself, must be real acting.

She recognized many of the faces she had seen on
Broadway and in movies. She pulled at Giulio's sleeve.
"There's Rosalind Cousins," she said, and she couldn't
keep herself from staring. She was even more beautiful
offstage than on, which was something Kate would never
have believed possible. Her hair was light brown with
coppery highlights, dressed in loose waves framing her
face and the huge, famous brown eyes. She wore an
Edwardian jacket of violet moiré silk with matching tai-
lored skirt and shoes. An intricate amethyst pendant hung
at her throat, and diamond studs winked in her ears. The
corners of her mouth turned up impishly as she listened
to a dark-haired man whispering into her ear.

"Would you like to meet her?" Giulio said.

"Meet her? Do you mean you know her?"

"Well enough to introduce you. Come on, don't be
shy."

Kate hung back. "Giulio, I couldn't."

"Of course you can. Don't be a ninny."

Giulio and Rosalind kissed the air beside each other's

cheeks, and the dark-haired man excused himself and left. Rosalind turned to Kate, and her cinnamon-colored eyes grew even larger.

"Giulio!" she cried. "Introduce me. You've found Mysterious Mimi, the Mad Mapper."

"As far as I know, this is Kate Elliot. Kate, Ros—"

"Where do you live?" Rosalind demanded.

"On West Fifty-sixth," said Kate. "In the building across from yours."

Rosalind's eyes narrowed in a parody of suspicion. "In the apartment across from mine, to be precise."

"Yes," Kate confirmed.

"How lovely to meet you at last. Giulio, we're old friends. We've been waving at each other for—"

"Four years," Kate supplied.

"Is it that long? Did you two go to the show tonight? I didn't see you there. I'm lending moral support to the director—we English have to stick together, you know—though I don't think he need worry; I thought the play was simply brilliant."

"No," said Giulio. "We didn't make the play." He laid a caressing hand on the back of Kate's neck.

"Who are you in aid of?"

"Don Ricci."

"Oh, he did gorgeous sets, breathtaking. The light people forgot a gel or something in Act Two, but don't tell him I noticed. Now," she said, taking Kate's hand, "you must come over here and sit with me and tell me what you do. I've been watching you—I'm shameless, I admit it. What *are* you doing over there? Giulio, the girl works like a maniac—day and night, night and day. She's as dedicated as a nun."

"She's not a nun," said Giulio in a decidedly lascivious tone, his warm hand sliding boldly down Kate's bare back.

Kate stepped, very carefully, on his patent leather toes.

"Giulio, darling," said Rosalind. "Are you in pain? You look like you're suffering from wind. You should take papaya enzyme tablets every morning. Why don't you fetch us something to drink and ask the barman for some bicarb?"

"I must tell you," said Kate, feeling like a gushing schoolgirl, "I think you're a wonderful actress."

"Thank you," said Rosalind in a solemn voice.

"I've seen all your plays since I came to New York."

"Have you? And which one did you like best?"

"I loved them all," Kate burst out. But it was true— she had.

"Bless you, darling. But tell me—since we two are waving neighbors, as it were, why have you never come backstage?"

"I've thought about it, but I've never had the nerve."

"A shy nun. Now I want to know what it is you're doing over there all day and half the night. You're some kind of artist, aren't you?"

"Yes, I illustrate and design books and jackets and covers and brochures and things," she finished up lamely. "I'm a free-lancer."

"Free-lancer. That sounds like you carry a spear in *Aïda* and come on following the camels, which must be better than following the elephants. And have I seen any of your books around?"

Kate named several that had been published in the last year.

"Then I *have* seen your work. You're very good."

Giulio returned with three glasses of champagne.

"Giulio, she's very good," said Rosalind.

"You don't have to tell me that," he said with an ever so masculine smirk.

"I meant as an artist, you beast!"

"You don't have to tell me that, either," he rejoined. "I've hired her."

"As a free spear?"

"Very free," he said, his eyes twinkling and his hand sliding down her back again. "What was all that nonsense about 'Mysterious Mimi'?"

Rosalind smiled slyly. "I must confess, excellent Kate, that I've made up rather a lot of stories about you. You're so mysterious, because when you're working I can see you only in profile. I have never—not even once—been able to see what you're working on. Well, that summer you moved in, you were hunched up for weeks on end with a tee-tiny pen in your hand, so I decided you did maps. Hence, Mysterious Mimi, the Mad Mapper."

Kate laughed, and Giulio gave her a loving hug. "I was doing medical illustrations for a drug company."

Giulio said, "Do you mean you two have been semaphoring to each other for four years, and you've never even tried to meet?"

They shook their heads.

"Silly, isn't it, that we haven't," said Rosalind, finishing her champagne. "Would you be an angel and bring me another?" she asked Giulio. The moment he left, she turned to Kate, lowering her voice to a conspiratorial whisper. "What have you done to Feral Fraser, the terror of every debutante's mother—the ruin of ingenues and ballerinas—"

"Well, I—"

"Kate, he's as meek as a lamb. I've been watching

him—he can't take his eyes off you...or his hands. He's positively doting."

"I'm very fond of him." Kate could feel her cheeks burning.

Rosalind cackled and leaned closer. "I've heard he's a divine cook. Is it true?"

"Here you are," said Giulio, handing Rosalind her champagne.

"That was quick, darling," Rosalind said waspishly, winking at Kate.

Kate winked back. "May I ask you a personal question?"

Rosalind sipped her champagne. "Possibly."

"What is your cat's name?"

Rosalind Cousins laughed her famous laugh. "Walter. His name is Walter." She subsided into fiendish giggles. "I don't know what I was expecting your question to be. Are you fond of cats? Would you like to meet him? He watches you, too, you know."

"I'd love to meet him," said Kate.

"Then you must come to tea one afternoon."

The dark-haired man returned to whisper in Rosalind's ear again.

"You must excuse me, darlings, I must rush. Remember, excellent Kate, you're coming to tea." And she disappeared into the crowd at the door.

"I'll never understand women," Giulio said with a snort. "Can you imagine two men waving at each other for four years across an airshaft? It would be ludicrous. And if I found myself living across the way from an actor whose work I admired, I'd make it a point to meet him and tell him so."

"I think women are more sensitive to each other's privacy."

"That's what we need now, darling." He touched one finger lightly to her lips. "Privacy. Let's go."

"It's much too early—we haven't heard the reviews yet."

A man carrying a plate of food asked if he might take one of the empty places at the table they'd just moved to. He introduced himself, but Kate was still thinking about Rosalind, and she missed his name. Though he was a tall man with a proud beak of a nose and the nasal twang of New England, his drooping gray mustache made him look like Pancho Villa's benevolent uncle.

"I don't know why I come to these things," he said. "An opening night party has all the charm of raising a last brave glass with the condemned, their eyes wide with terror, their ears straining for the clang of the tumbrel's iron wheels on the flinty cobbles of Forty-fourth Street." He munched cheerfully on a chicken leg.

"You're not an actor?" Kate queried. Giulio's leg pressed hers beneath the table. She smiled.

"No, my dear. My saturnine countenance cast its irresistibly melancholy spell over Broadway years ago, but no longer. I labor now in vineyards that do not yield the rich and soul-sustaining Burgundies of the theater, but, planted as they are on the lower slopes of meager, less sunny hills, yield but the less dramatic wines, the *vin ordinaire* of American life. In short, I write soap operas."

"Which one do you write?" Kate asked. Giulio's leg pressed harder, and her thigh was beginning to tingle.

"'Every Mother's Son.'"

"Really?" said Kate. "I always listen to the soaps while I work, though I can't really watch. Why did you kill off Emily just like that? It seemed so sudden. I really loved hating her."

"Ah, yes. Poor Emily. Agnes Calder, who played the

role, came down with an inner-ear disease and started reeling about the set like a drunken sailor, crashing into tables, falling over chairs. She had to check into an ear clinic. We couldn't replace her, so I let her drown in her health-club whirlpool. It seemed the most fitting end—death by water. Excuse me while I replenish my chicken."

Giulio said, "I really think it's time to—"

Suddenly the room fell silent, and all heads turned toward the door. A man with notes in his hand stood on a chair, waving with both arms. Giulio pressed her hand.

"We've got a winner!" the man shouted. "I've got the television reviews here. Segal, Lindstrom, and Lyons—they all loved it. We'll have the morning papers in another thirty mintues."

Everyone cheered and clapped and kissed one another.

Giulio kissed her soundly and long. "Kate, now?"

"But all the reviews aren't in. *The Times* and—"

"If we don't leave now, I intend to roll you under this table and have my way with you while that man eats his chicken over our heads."

"Well, if you put it like that . . . But I wonder what's become of your friend Don?"

As Giulio hustled her toward the exit, they met Don Ricci at the checkroom. After making hurried introductions, Giulio demanded, "Where have you been, Don? Did you hear the TV reviews? They're raves."

"Yeah, I heard. I've been at the theater going over the light plot. Did you see what they did to my second-act set? The bastards forgot a gel, and the whole thing looked green. Green! Oh, God, it was hideous!"

"Well, the critics didn't notice," Giulio soothed.

"What do they know?" Ricci moaned in despair.

"Congratulations," Kate said weakly.

"Yeah, thanks," he mumbled.

Soon they were alone on the street, and Kate hugged Giulio, saying, "How can I thank you for taking me to such a marvelous party?"

"I can think of a number of ways—all of which I intend to show you. Which will it be—your place or mine?"

"Mine, you fool. I'd hate to see my doorman's face if I came in at seven in the morning in an evening dress."

"What do you care what your doorman thinks?"

"You wouldn't understand, darling. You lads are all alike."

CHAPTER TWELVE

KATE LAY DREAMING. She and Giulio had been picnicking in the woods. He slept while she drowsed in his arms, wondering vaguely why, if she could plainly hear it raining, they weren't getting wet. She was about to waken him and ask what he thought about it when she heard the wretched animal's cry. It was a strangled wail that caught at her heart, but at the same time it sounded strangely joyous. She sat bolt upright in bed, her heart pounding, blinking herself awake.

Giulio was singing in the shower. He was singing "La donna è mobile" at heart-stopping volume, with flourishes, tender emotion, and manly exuberance—and outrageously off key. Kate buried her face in her pillow to stifle her laughter. She bit her knuckles, but that only made it worse. By the time he came back into the bedroom, still singing, she was doubled over, clutching her stomach, tears running down her cheeks.

"You must be the exception that proves the rule, darling," she said, giggling.

"And what rule is that, may I ask?" His voice was haughty, his bearing noble. Holding his chin high, he looked down his nose at her.

Kate wiped her streaming eyes. "There's an old Norwegian proverb: With money in your pocket, you are wise, you are handsome, and you can sing well, too," she improvised.

He cleared his throat with great dignity. "I take it you don't care for my singing."

This started her off on another fit of laughter. She gasped for breath. "Oh, my poor darling. Are you really Italian?"

"Si!"

She rubbed her eyes and sniffed the last laughing tears. "Go put on your clothes and I'll make coffee, such as it is."

"No time, my love. I have an early meeting."

"Won't you be a trifle overdressed wearing black tie?"

"I keep a change of clothes at the office. Now kiss me good-bye. I'll see you tonight." And then he was gone.

When she reached the kitchen, Kate found his note propped against the coffee pot. "Don't forget, Marple—eight o'clock, my place. I love you." Kate grinned. The note was signed, "Bond."

She carried her coffee to the couch, opened her date book, and began her morning round of telephone calls. Her California call she left until last because of the time difference. She had designed a new wine label for Jim Bennett's small winery in Sonoma. Bennett had called her late last night and left a message on her answering machine to call him ASAP. Just as she reached for the receiver, the phone rang.

It was Neal, and his tone was accusatory. "You haven't returned any of my calls."

"No."

"What have you been doing with yourself?"

"I've been very busy."

"I've really missed you, Kate. When can I see you?"

"I don't think we should see each other, Neal. I thought I made that clear before you went up to Albany to try your case. There's no future for us, Neal—unless you can accept my friendship, period."

"I didn't think you really meant it, I guess."

"I did, and I still do."

"Are you seeing someone else?"

"Yes, Neal, I am. I'm sorry, but I've been trying for a long time to make you understand that we're not right for each other."

"Won't you at least have dinner with me?" She could positively hear his chin wobbling.

"Neal, we've already spent hours and hours talking this over. You're a nice man, Neal, and I'll always be fond of you, but that's all." This could go on all morning if she didn't cut it off right now. "I must go now; I have to call California." And with a hurried good-bye, she hung up.

Kate dialed the number. "Mr. Bennett? This is Kate Elliot returning your call."

"I want you to know I like your label design," he said, "and so does my wife."

"Then what's the problem?" She could tell from his voice that something was worrying him.

"We've hired a new sales manager, and he...uh...he thinks it's too plain."

"I see."

"He brought in a bottle of Guten's Liebfraumilch. He says that's the kind of label we need. And you know that Guten's sells like crazy, and it's a terrible wine. Ours is much better."

"The label didn't sell that wine, Mr. Bennett. It was sold by an enormous campaign of radio ads. They spent a fortune on those ads. Don't you remember—they were very funny?"

"Yeah, you're right."

"If we put that sort of label on your bottles, no one will ever notice them on the shelves; they'll look like all the others. You might as well camouflage your wine."

"Yes, you're right, you're absolutely right!"

"That's what you're paying me for, Mr. Bennett."

After making a few more calls, Kate poured herself another cup of coffee, and Angela telephoned.

She sounded harried and urgent. "Kate, have you ever done any press checks?"

"Sure."

"How many? What kinds?"

"I've probably done dozens. Everything from one-color presses to five colors on a Web. Why?"

"Can you pack up some samples of the books you've done and a batch of your best covers and bring them right over?"

"Yes, of course, but why?"

"I'll tell you when you get here."

Kate hastily reorganized her day's priorities, gathered up her materials, rushed to Hill Press, and presented herself at her friend's office.

"Put your things here," said Angela. She had cleared a long table next to her desk. Kate emptied her portfolio onto the table and turned to the other woman. Angela looked haggard and worried, with lines of tension around her eyes.

She poured Kate a cup of tea from her bottomless pot. "Have you thought at all about the proposal I made the last time you were here, when I said I wanted to put your name up for art director?" She went right on before Kate could answer. "Everything's changed. I'm not leaving at the end of the year. I'm leaving as soon as I can."

"Why? What's happened?"

She didn't look at Kate; she looked at the papers on her desk. "I'm pregnant."

"Your fiancé hasn't—"

"Oh, no, nothing like that. We're getting married in three weeks. And that means I'll be leaving here as soon as I can break someone in. You're still my first choice for the job."

"Angela, I'm a graphic designer and an illustrator. I'm not an art director. Ian Fraser tried to talk me into joining his department, and I said no. That's not what I want to do. I don't want to give up free-lancing."

"Did Fraser offer you an art director's job or a job as an illustrator?"

"Illustrator."

"That's not the same thing, is it? Look, this isn't a huge department like his; we're a much smaller house. My staff designs the books, but we buy all our illustrations and covers from free-lancers. Rather than working *for* someone, you'd be *it*. There isn't a single aspect of my job you haven't done at one time or another—and done well. Now isn't that true?"

"Yes, I suppose it is."

"I was an illustrator when I took this job. The company was just starting out, and I brazened my way through. I faked it while I learned on the job. I knew a great deal less than nothing about things you know well enough to do in your sleep. Your experience is tailor-made for this job. You've worked with writers and editors, you're very good on typography, and the good lord knows you know how to buy art and photography. I'm sure you can manage the budgets; you know all about color separations and the problems of press checking. Kate, this is a terrific opportunity for you, and I'd like to see you get the same chance I did."

"Angela, I don't know what to say. When you first brought this up I told Fraser about it—I didn't tell him where—and he spent an entire lunch giving me fifty reasons why I should take the job."

"There! You see? And think about *this* for a minute: It would be *your* vision informing the entire line, *your* ideas. You may find this hard to believe, but they give me tremendous latitude here. Of course I'm answerable to marketing and accounting, but they both ask the same question: 'Will it sell books?'"

"I can't say it doesn't sound tempting, and at the end of the year I might have taken you up on it, but I'm buried by commitments now. I've just signed a contract with Fraser for two hundred drawings."

"Have you started on them?"

"No, we've just completed the photography."

"Then tell him you want out."

"I couldn't do that."

"Why not? It's done all the time. Will you at least talk to my boss before you make a decision?"

"Yes, but—"

Before Kate could say any more, Angela was out the door. She returned so quickly with two men in tow that Kate suspected they had been lurking in the hall.

Angela introduced them. Mr. Hill, the publisher, was

silver-haired and courtly; Bob Russell, his marketing director, was round-faced and smiling and looked young enough to be Hill's grandson. They went directly to the table on which Kate had spread her samples. For some minutes they looked through the work, murmuring to each other. Kate sat sipping nervously at her tea. Angela had discreetly disappeared.

Mr. Hill turned. "Miss Elliot, will you show us, please, which pieces you consider your best work?"

The younger man perched on the edge of the table; the publisher sat in Angela's chair. Kate picked out six things of which she was very proud.

"Yes," said Mr. Hill.

"Yup," said Bob Russell.

"Agreed, Bob?" Mr. Hill prompted.

"Absolutely," he said and, excusing himself, he left the office.

Mr. Hill smiled at Kate and stroked his smooth pink chin. "How long has Angela been buying work from you?"

"Six years."

"Bob and I are in complete agreement with Angela; you're the right person for her job. Now as for salary . . ."

Kate couldn't keep her eyes from widening when he quoted the salary and began describing the fringe benefits. He was deep in the labyrinthine intricacies of the company pension plan before Kate found her voice.

"Mr. Hill, I can't possibly make a decision today. I have to have some time to think about this. On top of which, as I've already told Angela, I have a contract with Talbot and Beach that I don't think I can get out of."

"Have you tried?" he asked gently.

"No. I've never done anything like that in my life."

"Have you actually started the job?"

"Just the preliminary work."

"I see. If you don't take this job—if you continue as a free-lancer—where do you expect you'll be in ten years? Have you given your future any serious thought?"

"I can't honestly say that I have. I've been so busy getting where I am now that I've never thought very far ahead. I've made a good name for myself, Mr. Hill; I win an award now and then."

"You don't have to defend yourself to me, Miss Elliot; I'm on your side. Free-lance work is fine when you're starting out, making a name for yourself, but there are several inherent dangers I'd like you to consider. Unless you work only for houses like ours that buy all their work outside, and unless you're a superstar, most of your work—not all, but most of it—will be overflow—the jobs other houses are too busy to handle themselves. Then, too, art directors are like casting directors—they typecast you. They hire you to do what they know you've done before. They don't give you any challenges, anything new that would really stretch your creative muscles. They want what you did for them the last time around. Haven't you begun to find that?"

Kate smiled in agreement. He sounded so like Giulio.

"If you work for me, I guarantee you'll discover creative muscles you didn't even know you had." He stood up and extended his hand. His palm was warm and his eyes were kind. "Will you think about what I've said, and if you're interested, will you try to void that contract and call me by Friday afternoon?"

"Thank you, Mr. Hill, I will think about it, and I'll call you."

He left the office, and Angela returned to pop back

into her desk chair, the two of them changing places with the precision of figures on a Swiss weather clock.

"That man is heaven to work for," Angela commented.

Kate began repacking her portfolio. "I told him I'd call him by Friday, but Angela, I just don't see how I can do it. And I'm still not sure I want to."

"You have so much potential, Kate. I know—I've gone through the portfolio of every designer in New York who can grip a pencil; you wouldn't believe some of the work I've seen. I know it's a cliché, but this is the chance of a lifetime for you." She took both of Kate's hands in her own. "None of us can get very far without some help. I know how hard you've worked, but you can't do it all on your own. You've come this far; now let me help."

Kate thanked Angela and made her way out of the building. Lost in thought, blind to the jostling crowds around her, she walked slowly uptown. It was true that if she took the job, she would be able to do more, creatively, than she was doing now. Mr. Hill was right about that. She could all too easily imagine herself in ten years, in twenty years, still hoping for choice crumbs and crusts to fall from art directors' abundant boards, making the most of them, preening over an occasional award. Who was she kidding, she asked herself. The salary was nearly twice what she made now. There would be time and money enough to spend on the place in Woodstock.

How could she talk Giulio into letting her out of that contract? Would it mean the end of their relationship? Why should it, she asked herself. He was a compassionate man. He said he loved her. He'd have to see what an incredible opportunity this was for her. He wouldn't stand in her way; he wasn't that sort of man.

And he'd said himself that she should take the job. He'd probably cheer me on, she decided. Give her a kiss and a hug and take her out for a smashing lunch to celebrate.

Filled with happy expectation, she hailed a cab and rode the rest of the way to Giulio's office. She would be able to take real vacations. She could go to Italy with Giulio. She imagined the two of them sitting in a sidewalk café in Florence. The setting was slightly out of focus, because she had never been to Florence—*Firenze,* she corrected herself—but the foreground, with Giulio and the love in his laughing eyes, was very clear.

Giulio met her at his office door. "Darling, what are you doing here? I thought you were home, slaving away." He kissed her lightly. "Sit down and tell me why you've come."

Begin positively, she told herself. "I've decided to take your advice," she said.

"What advice?"

"I've been offered Angela Rogers's job at Hill Press." Warily she watched his eyes.

"The art director's job? Are you going to take it?"

"Yes, if I can."

His eyes were warm. "Good for you! This calls for a celebration." He paused. "What do you mean, *if* you can?"

"I'd have to start almost immediately. Angela's leaving to get married."

His eyes turned cold. "But you can't start that soon; you have my drawings to do."

She felt her stomach clench into a fist, and she took a deep breath. "I know. I'll need your help. I'd like you to cancel our contract."

"You must be joking." His face was a mask now, as cold as his eyes. "I won't do that. I can't do that—not after all I went through getting the money boys to agree to a royalty for you."

"What would you have done if I hadn't agreed to do this job? You must have had someone else in mind in case I turned you down."

"You've signed a contract, Kate." His tone was menacing.

"But you could talk them into canceling it as easily as you talked them into making it."

"I doubt it. And even if I could, that's beside the point. I want *your* drawings, not someone else's. I want the best book possible—that's my responsibility. I won't settle for second-class work."

"You're exaggerating, darling. I'm not the only illustrator in New York. The woods are full of artists who could draw Gunilla."

He said nothing. His face was expressionless, but she could see a vein pulsing in the center of his forehead. Why was he being so unreasonable? She tried to keep her voice level and calm. "Be sensible. The photos are done; I directed them. You can have that work gratis. There must be someone you could hire—"

The mask broke. His face turned dark with anger. "How can you do this to me?"

"Why to you? Why not to the company? This isn't personal, Giulio, you must know that. You sound like a petulant child."

"A child? *I* sound like a child? It's time you grew up. This is the real world, where obligations are met—in this case your obligation to me and my obligation to Talbot and Beach. Until you understand that, you'll never be a professional."

"And what about me? My obligation to myself? You're the one who's been telling me I need to take on new challenges, greater responsibilities. You're the one who gave me the grand lecture on Kate Elliot, her talent and how to nurture it."

"I never imagined your doing it at my expense." He stood staring out the window.

Why wouldn't he look at her, she wondered. Why wouldn't he help her? She would not plead with him. There had to be a way to get through to him. "Giulio, I believed all those things you said about how careers are made, how they don't just happen. This is my chance. Is your one book more important than my entire career? Why do you care about it so much?"

"Because that's my job," he spat back. "How do you think you can be an art director if you don't understand where your loyalties belong? My first responsibility is to my line—my books. Insisting on you is a matter of aesthetic judgment. I know what I want that book to look like, and I will not settle for less."

"In other words you're not letting me out of my contract."

He turned to face her, flecks of light glinting in his eyes like ice. His voice was low, his tone dispassionate, dismissing, and stacatto. "No. I'm not letting you out. Of anything. Get out of here. Go home. And start working."

The fist in her stomach hurt so much she could hardly breathe. "And I thought you loved me," she said bitterly.

"This is business, Kate. Love doesn't enter into it. You ought to know that."

She got up to leave, turning to him as she stood in the doorway, "The only thing I know is that you are an arrogant bastard!"

CHAPTER THIRTEEN

"I'VE REALLY DONE it this time!" Kate said aloud, pitching her portfolio toward the corner behind her front door. It slid down the wall and slapped against the floor. Why had she let her temper get the best of her like that? There was no way he'd ever change his mind now—not after an exit line like that. How could she have been such a damn fool as to imagine that Fraser the Great might defer to her, might care about her interests? And there she'd been, planning romantic vacations for two in Firenze. *Firrrrenze!* Idiot! She'd be lucky to get to New Jersey.

Whatever lingering reservations Kate might have had about taking the art director's job were forgotten now, buried beneath hurt and fury. Legal advice, she thought, that's what I need. She grabbed the phone and dialed Neal's number.

His voice was eager, and she felt rotten for getting his hopes up.

"Kate," he said. "What an unexpected pleasure."

"I'm calling for some free legal advice, Neal. Do you have a minute to talk?"

"I always have time for you—you know that."

She winced. "I've signed a contract, with Talbot and Beach, for some drawings. It's a royalty contract. Is there any way I can get out of it, short of an act of God?"

"You must understand that I can't make any sort of informed judgment without reading the contract, but if it's a standard publisher's contract, a typical instrument, no. You're locked in, unless you're willing to undertake some expensive litigation. Why do you want out?"

"It's too complicated to explain right now, but thank you anyway."

"Would you like me to read over the contract? I might find something. Why don't we have dinner tonight and go over it?"

"No, thank you, Neal."

"I'm sorry I can't be more helpful."

"Thanks anyway."

Kate worked mechanically through the rest of the day, but her thoughts kept returning to Giulio and her blighted plans. His attitude had verged on vindictiveness. Why, she wondered. Did he think she was rejecting him and not his contract? Why was she making excuses for him? If he really cared for her as much as she cared for him, he would have found a way out for her.

Her brooding was interrupted by the ringing phone. She glanced at her watch: six o'clock. Could he have changed his mind? She let the bell ring four times before she answered.

"Kate, this is Jeffrey. Are you all right?" He sounded hesitant but concerned.

"I'm fine," she lied.

"What happened? After you stalked out like a raging Rhine maiden, Giulio came steaming out of his office and stood over my drawing board, breathing fire on my Magic Markers. What did you say to him?"

"I told him I'd been offered the art director's job at Hill Press."

"But Kate, that's marvelous."

"No, it's not. I can't have the job unless I can start soon, and that means I can't do your drawings. But Giulio won't help me get out of the contract."

"I see."

"I know you two could find another illustrator, but he won't even try."

"Then maybe I can help. When Gunilla's book was in the planning stage, the marketing department wanted photographs, not drawings. I don't think Giulio ever really convinced them—he just wore them down by talking longer and louder."

"He's good at that."

"I think Melissa's photos of Gunilla are extraordinary, don't you?" He didn't wait for an answer. "Let's suppose marketing just happened to see those pics—accidentally, you understand. They'd be climbing all over Giulio to cancel your contract and use Melissa's stuff instead. He'd never be able to talk them out of it."

"But Jeffrey, he'll be furious with you. I can't let you go out on a limb like that for me. That's the sort of hanky-panky that gets designers fired."

"Dear child, Giulio will never know I arranged it. It will be the simplest thing in the world to stage-manage."

"I'd be so grateful, Jeffrey. Are you sure you're not going to get yourself in trouble? I have to give Hill my answer on Friday."

"No problem. Trust me. I'll call you."

* * *

In slow motion, trying not to hope, Kate managed to work through Wednesday, but by Thursday her concentration had deserted her. She spent most of her time pacing the length of her small living room, from the door to the windows and back to the door. She watched "As the World Turns," "General Hospital," and "Every Mother's Son," and she wondered what had happened to the actress with the ear problem. "Ring!" she shouted at the telephone. "Why don't you ring?" And it promptly rang.

She took two deep breaths, letting the air out slowly, and lifted the receiver with a trembling hand. Her throat tightened.

"Hello?" she said, swallowing hard.

"Kate? This is Rosalind Cousins. Are you all right? Would you like to come over for a cup of tea?"

"Oh, Miss Cousins." Suddenly Kate could breathe again.

"Did I call at a bad time? Would you rather not?"

"No, I'd love to come." It would do her good to get out, and if Jeffrey called, he'd leave a message on her machine.

"I've been watching you pacing and prowling like a caged thing," said Rosalind. "I thought a cup of tea might help. Come in and meet Walter." She scooped the ginger cat up into her arms. "Walty, this is Kate, your admirer from across the way."

Walter looked skeptical but graciously allowed Kate to rub his ears and scratch the top of his head.

"I think he knows who you are, but he doesn't understand why you're here and not there."

A kettle whistled from the kitchen. "Why don't you take that chair," said Rosalind. "I'll bring our tea."

Kate found herself in a cozy English sitting room so perfectly rendered it reminded her of the miniature period rooms at the Chicago Art Institute. There was a Queen Anne desk and an intricately inlaid Boulle table. Needlepoint cushions were strewn on the biscuit-colored sofa and in the matching wing chairs. The paintings were English landscapes in gilt frames. Kate wondered idly where Rosalind kept her acting awards.

Rosalind returned with a tea tray, a plate of cookies, another of sliced cake, and a saucer of sausage slices.

"Do you take your tea with milk and sugar, or do you prefer lemon?" said Rosalind.

"Milk and sugar will be fine. That's how my mother always drank it, so I do too."

"It's been rather a comfort to me having you across the way all these years."

"It has?" Kate was incredulous.

"No matter how depressed I might be, I know I can look over and see you carrying on so brightly at whatever you might be doing, never flagging, always beetling on with it, and it always cheers me up. I say to myself, Coz, get on with it! If Mimi can keep on mapping, there is still sanity in this world. Though the past two days you've looked positively *distrait,* my dear. Would you like to tell me about it, or would you rather we drink our tea, eat our biscuits, and I'll shut up?"

This was not what Kate had anticipated—she had imagined an hour of theatrical anecdotes amusingly recounted by a Great Lady of the Theater.

"I don't mind talking about it, but I don't really know where to begin."

"Try the beginning. Would you like a cigarette?"

"Desperately, but I've quit."

"How I envy you! I wish I could. Now, the beginning," she said, lighting a cigarette and blowing plumes of smoke through her nose.

"Giulio Fraser hired me to illustrate a book for him . . . and somewhere along the way we fell in love."

"I suspected something of the sort." Rosalind fed Walter a slice of sausage.

"I had thought I would always go on as a free-lancer, just as I have been, but he convinced me that it would be much better for my career if I took an art director's job I was offered. The position was supposed to come open in about nine months. Well, the job didn't wait that long. It came my way Tuesday, the day before yesterday."

"That's rather short notice, isn't it?"

"It was sort of an emergency. I can't take the job if Giulio won't let me out of my contract. I really want that job—it's a terrific chance—and I thought he'd be all for it. But we had a terrible fight, and he said he wouldn't do it."

"He *can* have an evil temper."

"He was raging like an ogre—all high and mighty, no sensitivity. He said loving me didn't enter into it— that this was business. It was awful. His chief designer is trying to help me behind the scenes, without Giulio's knowing it. It's his call I've been waiting for. I have to say yes or no to the job offer tomorrow, and the waiting has been driving me crazy."

"And at this moment you're so angry with Giulio you can't see straight."

"Yes, I am, and he knows it. I called him an arrogant bastard, I'm afraid."

"Did you indeed?"

"I don't know how I let myself get into this situation. I've always made it a rule never to date the men I work with—and to steer clear of his type of domination. Somehow he got under my defenses."

"Hmm," she said, nibbling at a piece of cake. "I'm sure it's every bit as unsatisfactory as falling in love with your director. That's utter disaster, darling. No matter how much they say they love you, when it comes to *their* play, you might as well be a one-line walk-on—to bloody hell with being the star."

"That's how Giulio is: with him, it's *his* book, *his* requirements, *his* everything! Kate Elliot definitely takes a backseat on *his* ego trip."

"How serious was it between you two?"

"He wanted me to move in with him."

"Did he, now? The sly puss. And what did you say?"

"I said I'd think about it."

"I don't believe he's ever asked anyone else to do that."

"What makes you think so?"

"Because no one ever has. As you yourself so readily admit, he usually gets what he asks for. And remember, I've known him for a long time. He's eminently eligible; the sort of man women talk about and the gossip columnists pick up on. I'm sure I would have heard." She poured out the last of the tea and fed Walter the last piece of sausage. "Kate, I don't think you should write him off yet. If he's proposing a live-in arrangement, he must be very serious."

"It doesn't matter now," she said miserably. "At this moment I don't think I could even see my way clear to forgiving him. And one thing I don't need in my life right now is a domineering prig who requires subservience at all costs."

Rosalind smiled. "I know, but your anger will pass."

"It's hard to believe," Kate said dubiously.

"Will you call me when you find out about the contract—one way or the other?" She wrote her telephone number on a slip of paper and handed it to Kate.

"Yes, I will. You've been very kind to have me over like this," Kate said.

"Nonsense. We women have to stick together. Men are such hell, aren't they? We can't live with 'em, and we can't live without 'em."

"I don't know. Right now I think I'm ready to become the Drawing Nun."

When Kate's phone rang Thursday night, her heart dropped to the pit of her stomach and lay there like a cold stone.

"You can take the job, Kate!" Jeffrey crowed.

Her heart thumped, and she was flooded with relief. "What happened?"

"It didn't go the way I'd planned—I never had a chance to do my number. The marketing man came down and said he'd heard I had some pretty good photos of Gunilla. So I hauled them out and did my show-and-tell. Then he walked into Giulio's office and stayed for about two minutes. Then he left. Then Giulio rang my phone and said marketing had prevailed—we'd be using Melissa's photos, not your drawings."

"Oh, Jeffrey," she said, laughing with relief, "you've saved my life."

"Glad to be of help, but I really didn't do much—I didn't get a chance to. Good luck, Kate. Give me a call when you get settled in at Hill and let me know how it's going. And if there's ever anything I can do to help, call me."

"Jeffrey, you're an angel. I will."

It was too late to call Mr. Hill; that would have to

wait until morning. She tried Marion, but she was out. Rosalind would be at the theater at this hour. She sat down at her drawing table and worked out a schedule for accounts whose work she would have to complete before or soon after starting her new job.

By the time she went to bed that night, the elation she had felt after Jeffrey's call had evaporated. She stared at the ceiling, wondering why it had had to happen like this. Why did she feel as if she'd traded Giulio for the brass ring?

At eight o'clock the next morning a messenger handed her a manila envelope with the Talbot and Beach logo in the corner. It was their copy of her contract. Scrawled across the blue cover was the message, "You'll be a fine A. D.—G."

Tears stung her eyes. "I've won," she whispered, "but I've lost."

CHAPTER FOURTEEN

For her first week at Hill Press, Kate sat at Angela's elbow thinking she was never going to be able to keep track of everything. By the middle of the following week, she found she could anticipate Angela's moves before she made them. Her third Monday began her first week alone on the job, and she called her Monday morning staff meeting with a feeling of unfeigned confidence.

The afternoon was given over to an editorial conference. Editors presented recently acquired books, discussing with Bob Russell from marketing and with Kate their ideas on how each of the books should be handled. Everything seemed to go smoothly until Ginnie Shaw came to the last book of the afternoon.

"When Martine Doineaux retired from fashion modeling," Ginnie began, "she was the highest paid model in the business. As some of you may know, she promptly opened her own modeling agency, and it's been enormously successful. This is her autobiography, as told to Stephen Gould, of course."

"Of course," said Jay Briggs, who edited fiction.

Ginnie pointedly ignored him. "She has masses of photos we can use. I thought two sixteen-page signatures of them, with the last eight pages reserved for shots of her now—at home, running her agency, that sort of thing. It's a very uplifting story of a woman who refused to go off to the boneyard. It'll be a great shot in the arm for working women who are worrying about the advancing years. Doineaux talks candidly about her depression after she quit modeling and how by opening her agency, she found a way to go on doing what she'd done before, but to do it differently."

"Sounds good," said Bob. "Thirty-two pages of pictures will be great. And a shot of her today for the cover, don't you think, Kate?"

"Oh, yes," said Kate. "I know Melissa Edwards did a lot of her shots for *Vogue* and *Elle*. She's the obvious choice for the cover and interior shots."

Ginnie was reluctant to agree, for no reason Kate could imagine. "Pehaps someone else would do just as well," she posited.

"Who could be better? There would certainly be continuity in using her," Kate reasoned.

"That's true, Kate," Bob agreed.

Ginnie was dismissive. "Well, we don't have to come to a decision on this today, do we?"

"We should decide soon," said Kate, "if we hope to get into Melissa's booking schedule."

The following morning a gentle young man who had been recommended by Ginnie showed Kate his fashion photography. She paged carefully through his sample book, giving each picture her full attention. His work was technically competent but unoriginal. This must be what Simon's fashion stuff had been like, she mused. She thanked the young man for coming in. Then she called Ginnie, wondering what she was trying to do to her book.

"I've just seen your protégé's samples, Ginnie. They're capable enough, but awfully derivative. I really think Melissa would be far better for us."

"He'd be a lot cheaper," Ginnie pointed out.

"Melissa won't put us over budget. I'm as concerned as you must be that this book be as good as it possibly can. You know as well as I do that Melissa Edwards is just as big a name as Avedon or Penn or Hiro—and just as glamorous. Her work is light-years beyond that nice young man's who was just in here. I can't see any reason to settle for less than the best."

"Okay, okay," said Ginnie. "I simply thought I'd try to give the kid a leg up. He's a friend of a friend."

"I'll keep him in mind for future needs—how's that?"

"Thanks, Kate." They hung up.

"My God," Kate muttered to herself, "I sounded just like Giulio." She'd been protecting her own turf: worrying over what Ginnie was trying to do to her—Kate's—book, insisting on Melissa because she had to have the best. She'd been saying and thinking all those things he'd said to her—thinking like an art director. She really owed the man an apology for calling him a bastard when he was only doing his job and she was trying to welsh on a contract.

Nuts to that! She wasn't the only one who was wrong. Where was all that love and understanding and equality he'd gone on about? What happened to all that concern about her life and career? But why did she still miss him so? She shook her head and squared her shoulders, but the work in front of her kept swimming out of focus.

At noon, Kate left her office, a small layout pad tucked under her arm, and headed for the park. It was a radiant June day. She found a sunny bench, opened her pad, and began sketching two young men picnicking on the grass. She could feel the tension drain from her as she gave all her attention to her drawing.

A camera shutter clicked, and there stood the Edwards twins, grinning at her.

"I've taken your picture," said Polly. "Do you mind?"

"No, of course not," Kate assured her.

"Are you drawing those guys?" asked Rick, pointing to the picnickers.

Kate showed them her drawing.

"That's very good," Rick said solemnly.

"Would you draw me?" Polly asked.

"Sit on the end of the bench," Kate directed, turning to a fresh page. Deftly she sketched the child, one leg pulled up on the bench, her chin on her knee, the camera around her neck, a look of grave expectancy in her eyes. Kate tore out the page and handed it to her.

"That was fast," said Rick in obvious awe.

"Oh, I specialize in fast," Kate said, smiling.

"May I keep it?" Polly couldn't take her eyes from the drawing.

Kate nodded.

"Will you come to our birthday party?" Rick asked. "It's a week from Friday night."

"Please say you'll come," Polly urged, looking up at last. "It's at seven-thirty."

"I'd love to come," said Kate.

"Great!" Polly said. "It's not very formal; you can

wear anything," she assured Kate, already the careful hostess.

"I'll keep that in mind."

"We have to go now," Rick said. "We're meeting Daddy at that photo gallery over on Lex." Shouting good-byes, they ran down the path and out of the park.

Kate watched them until they disappeared. Her eyes filled with tears, and she realized that all the anger she had been storing up was gone now. All that remained was regret and an overwhelming sense of loss. It was one of those dreams that was never meant to be, that was all, she told herself. But she could not imagine ever again feeling that special closeness she had felt with Giulio. Her tears splashed onto her folded hands.

Sorrowfully she walked back to her office, wondering what she should buy the twins for their birthday. She couldn't go empty-handed. Only then did it occur to her to wonder if Giulio would be there. Probably, she decided. After all, he was their godfather. She sighed. She'd have to apologize politely, and that would be the end of it.

When she reached her office, she found a neat pile of pink message slips her secretary had left in the center of her desk. Two were from Jeffrey Stewart.

She immediately returned his calls, and Jeffrey's voice was bubbling with excitement. "How's the new job going, Kate?"

"How nice of you to call, Jeffrey. It's fine. The first couple of weeks were rough, but I like my staff—I didn't inherit any deadwood—and everyone here is very easy to work with. What can I do for you?"

"My dear, it's what I can do for you. I had a fascinating tête-à-tête with Evelyn from our marketing department over lunch an hour ago."

Kate's voice rose in disbelief. *"You* lunched with marketing?"

"Research, dear. I've been trying to find out how marketing learned about those photos before they saw them. Evelyn, after being plied with two martinis, a crabmeat salad, and a half-bottle of Pouilly-Fuissé, confessed to me—on condition that I promised never to reveal it to a living soul at Talbot and Beach—which I'm not, because you're there, not here—"

"What did she say?"

"She told me that the day after you walked out of here, Giulio went in and told her boss that he, Giulio, had been wrong, that photographs were really a better idea than drawings for the *Body Book*, that Melissa had already taken them, and that they were perfect."

"He said he was wrong?"

"There's more. He and marketing set it up for marketing to casually wander in here and ask to see the pictures. But—and here's the kicker—Giulio asked him not to tell anyone he'd talked to him about it. Giulio wanted it to appear to be marketing's own decision so that, quote, he wouldn't look like a silly ass to his own department, unquote. In other words, he didn't want me to know, because he probably figured I'd tell you. Isn't that the damnedest thing? Giulio was in there pitching for you the whole time!"

"But why didn't he want me to know?"

"My dear, I can't imagine. You'll have to ask *him* that."

"Thank you for calling me, Jeffrey. I owe you one."

For a full minute Kate sat with her hand on the receiver, trying to make up her mind. Then she called Giulio.

* * *

Kate ordered a Perrier with lime and waited. She poked around in the bowl of salted nuts, picking out the cashews, and suddenly Giulio was sliding into the booth across from her.

"Hello, Kate," he said softly, folding his hands on the table between them.

She closed her eyes and instantly imagined his hands caressing her breasts, stroking her thighs. This was a mistake, she thought. She should have said everything over the phone. Why was she putting herself through this?

"How's your job going?" he asked. "Do you like it as much as you thought you would?"

"It's going very well. I'm learning a lot."

"Would you like another drink?"

She nodded. His eyes revealed nothing. His voice was cool, his manner reserved.

As the drinks arrived, he came to the point, "Why did you want to see me?"

In spite of his frigid politeness, Kate could sense he was holding himself in check. She felt like a hunter, picking her way through his careful conversation, wary of ambush, looking for clues—in his voice and his eyes and his mouth—for a sign that his love still existed, somewhere, buried beneath his chilling calm. Could she find her way back to that secure place where they had sheltered in each other's love?

"I owe you an apology—" she began.

"You don't—"

"Strictly speaking, I owe you two."

He leaned back, folding his arms across his chest, stretching out his long legs beneath the table.

Since taking her new job, Kate was feeling more in control of her own life than she ever had before. She knew she was stronger and more self-possessed, yet, much as she longed to, she couldn't find the strength to reach out and touch him. Instead she said, "I haven't had my job very long, but it's changed my perspective on things. This morning I heard myself defending my choice of Melissa over another photographer, for all the same reasons you once gave me. You were right, and I was wrong—and I wanted to tell you that. You were being completely professional, and I wasn't."

"You would have learned that sooner or later."

"That's not the only thing I learned today."

"Oh?" One eyebrow shot up.

"You got me out of that contract, didn't you?"

He shifted uncomfortably in his seat. "What makes you think—?"

"I know all about it, Giulio."

He reached for his wallet. "Let's get out of here."

"But I want to talk."

"And I want to walk. We should be able to manage both." He slapped several bills down onto the table and headed for the door.

Kate caught up with him on the sidewalk and grabbed his arm to slow him down. "Why couldn't you tell me what you did?" She felt his arm tensing beneath her hand.

"I really don't know." He glanced down into her eyes and as quickly looked away. "I know how important it is for you to feel independent, and I can't blame you for fighting for what you wanted—I would have done the same thing at your age."

Kate pulled on his arm, forcing him to stop walking and face her. "You would have?"

"You're damn right! It took a lot of guts for you to face me down like that. I like that, Kate."

"Oh, my darling! And I thought you'd given up on

me." She threw her arms around his neck and stood on
tiptoe, pressing herself against him. His late-afternoon
beard was harsh against her cheek, and she felt again the
tingling electric charge crackling up and down her spine.

"Dear Kate," he said at last, "my love for you had
everything to do with holding you to your contract.
Somewhere in the back of my mind I really believed that
someday we'd work together... and live together..."

"Giulio, please—"

"But when you decided to take that job at Hill, I
suddenly thought I was losing you."

"How could you think that? You know how I felt."
She touched his cheek, and he quickly turned his face
to kiss her palm.

"I guess I wasn't really sure," he confessed. "After
all, your drive for independence was always your longest
suit. So I didn't know what to say, I didn't know what
to do. If I held you to the contract, I was afraid I'd lose
you. If I let you go, I thought I'd lose you. I couldn't
win either way."

"You couldn't lose me, darling."

He gathered her hands into his. "This is too important
to talk about on the street. Let's go back to my office;
it's only five minutes from here." He kissed her hands.
"Please."

"All right," Kate said breathily.

With Giulio pulling her along swiftly, they made it
in three minutes. "Hold my calls," he commanded his
secretary as they flew past into his office. Panting, Kate
leaned against the inside of his closed door.

She could hear the hum of muted voices, the faint
ping of a typewriter bell, Jeffrey's piping laugh. Then
Giulio reached behind her, and the click of the lock

resounded like a rifle shot.

"Giulio, we must talk—" she began, but his lips took her words away as he crushed her against him, his kisses thrilling her with their hunger.

"I love you, Kate," he whispered. "I need you." His hands moved to her breasts.

"What are you doing?" she gasped, astonished by his boldness. "This is your office!"

"Yes," he murmured, opening her blouse. "My office. My delicious Kate. I'm going to love you, Kate."

"Not here!" she protested. "You can't do this here— and we have so much to talk about—we must..." But the reckless urgency of his passion excited her wildly, and she knew she could never have enough of his coaxing hands and playful fingers, his lips that alternately begged and ravaged, his pillaging tongue. She moaned as his mouth found her breast.

"Shh!" he warned, but he growled deep in his throat.

A knock exploded like a rocket just behind her ear. "Someone's out there!" she whispered, horrified, pushing him away.

"Dammit to hell!"

"Do you have a minute, Giulio?" Jeffrey sang out.

Hastily Kate pulled her clothes together and threw herself into a chair.

"Yes?" Giulio snapped, opening the door.

Jeffrey bustled in with an armful of proofs. "I have that color signature for you—the whole thing's hanging three dots out. Why, hello, Kate. You're looking delightfully flushed and eager. Your job must be agreeing with you." He dropped the proofs onto Giulio's desk. "I'll leave this mess with you."

Giulio closed the door and dropped into his chair.

"I'm sorry," he said, plunging his hands through his hair. "Where my feelings for you are concerned, I lose all judgment—"

"So do I, I'm afraid—"

"I lose control. It must be because I love you so much. Like my going to marketing for you—that was something I'd never have done before I met you. I still can't believe I did it."

"What do you mean?" she asked carefully, an unpleasant suspicion rearing its head.

"I allowed my personal feelings to get in the way of my professional responsibility. I intervened for personal reasons," he explained distractedly.

Anger pulled her to her feet, and she stared at him in disbelief. "I can't believe what I'm hearing. Are you saying you *sold out* for me?"

"I don't think I'd put it quite like that."

"Why not? *Sold out*—it's a useful phrase. Do you think you sold out?"

He folded his hands and studied the knuckles. "Yes, I suppose I do, and it's been a very hard thing for me to accept. But I didn't do it just for you; I couldn't have lived with myself if I'd held you to that contract. That's why I didn't call you—I'm been trying to sort all this out." He came around the desk and tried to take her hands, but she shoved them into her pockets.

"Sort what out? That you've tarnished your shining self-image? What are you—some kind of angel in a tweed jacket who's fallen from grace? Well, welcome to the human race, Mr. High-and-Mighty Fraser. We do things for each other all the time down here."

"I knew you wouldn't understand."

"You're right. I don't. How can you stand there wrapping yourself in righteousness and crooning over your guilt? You intervened because you love me. Why is that so terrible?"

His hands closed on her shoulders. "I want you back, Kate."

"I love you, Giulio. I'll probably always love you. But we can't start over if you see me as the evil genie for whom you besmirched your sacred honor. You're not Lancelot, and I'm not Guinevere. I don't want a knight in shining armor. I want a man! A man full of life and fire, who makes love like no one else on earth, who turns a hunk of veal into ambrosia in the blink of an eye, and who buys six toothbrushes at a time."

He stood stony-faced.

She pressed her hands against his chest, pushing herself away from him. "Call me when you're ready to hang up your suit of mail."

CHAPTER FIFTEEN

It was going to be a gorgeous day, Kate decided—perfect for driving up to the country. Yawning, she stretched and carried her morning coffee to the living room window. Walter sat on his windowsill, blinking into the sun. Her lobby buzzer sounded, and she glanced at her watch. Who would come over at seven o'clock on a Saturday morning?

"There's a messenger down here with a package for you," crackled the doorman.

"For me? On Saturday?"

"That's what he says. Do you want I should send him up?"

"Please." She had finished all her free-lance assignments. It must be some absentminded typesetter with a rush order who forgot that someone else was now handling one of her old accounts.

"I'm sorry to bring this so early," said the messenger, handing her a small box, "but the dispatcher said no later than seven. Sign here."

"Who is it from?"

"I dunno."

Kate closed the door and examined the package. This wasn't from any typesetter, she realized. It was the wrong shape. It was a white cardboard box no more than eight inches square, sealed with tape. Her name and address were printed in anonymous block capitals. There was no return address. Kate shook the box next to her ear: something thunked heavily inside. Was this somebody's idea of a joke, she wondered, slitting the tape with her thumbnail. Inside was another box, but this one was light blue, with TIFFANY & CO. printed on the lid. "No," she whispered to herself, "this is no joke." She took a deep breath and sat down.

Nestled deep within layers of crackling tissue lay a black suede drawstring pouch. Her fingers tore at the cords, but her hands trembled so violently she couldn't open them. She felt in the box for a card. She shook out each piece of tissue. There was no card. She finally pried the drawstring loose and held in her hand a gleaming silver replica of a knight in shining armor.

"Oh, Giulio," she said aloud, her heart aching with love. Despite everything she had said, she did feel like Guinevere.

At exactly seven-fifteen the phone rang. Kate sniffed back her tears and spoke first. "It's beautiful, Giulio. I'm overwhelmed."

"I'd like to start over, Kate." His voice sounded harsh and tight in his throat. "Do you think we could go back to the beginning?"

"No, not the beginning. Let's start from today . . . Are you all right? You sound terrible—like your throat's full of crushed ice."

"I haven't slept since you walked out of my office Tuesday."

"That's three nights!"

"I know," he said mournfully.

"Would you like to come with me to Woodstock? I'm going up there today."

"Are you staying with your friends?" There was a distinct lack of enthusiasm in his tone.

Kate laughed at his reluctance to have other people around. "No, we'll be alone. I finally arranged to buy my old wreck of a house."

"Perfect. How were you planning to get there?"

"I'm renting a car."

"Couldn't be better. Pick me up at my place in an hour and a half." He hung up.

Giulio was waiting on his doorstep when Kate pulled up. He stood knee-deep in wicker baskets and hampers.

"What's all that?" she asked incredulously, opening the trunk.

"Food. What did you plan to eat up there?"

"I thought I'd stop at the market for steaks or hamburgers when we got there."

"That's what I suspected," he said, arranging the hampers in the trunk. "This basket goes on the backseat. Would you like me to drive?"

She handed him the keys gratefully. Four cars were lined up behind them on the narrow street, their horns blaring angrily.

"Do you mind if we don't take the tunnel?" she asked. "I hate the tunnel."

Now that they were together, Kate felt unaccountably shy. Giulio was scrupulously polite. They drove uptown and across the George Washington Bridge, then headed north on the Palisades Parkway.

"I haven't thanked you properly for the beautiful silver knight."

"I meant it as a kind of pledge, a promise."

"I know." Kate wanted desperately to touch him, to break the tension. He was holding the steering wheel so tightly his knuckles shone white. Kate worried a dime-sized hole in her wheat-colored jeans with her thumb.

"Would you like the window open?" he asked, looking straight ahead.

"Yes, that would be nice."

He rolled his window down. "Is that too windy?"

"No, that's fine. Do you mind if I turn on the radio?"

"No, not at all."

She twisted the dial. It came off in her hand. "Well, so much for rented cars," she said. "I should buy a secondhand one—nothing grand, just reliable enough to get me up to Woodstock and back—but I don't know the first thing about cars."

"Would you like me to help you pick one out? I'm no expert, but I do know an air filter from a distributor cap. What kind do you think you'd like?"

"A red one."

He chuckled, and the tension dropped by one very small degree.

The hole in her jeans was now the size of a nickel. "Giulio, I can't stand this another minute! We're behaving like a couple of porcupines."

"Porcupines?"

"Yes, porcupines. Don't you know how porcupines make love?"

"No," he said, smiling now. "How do porcupines make love?"

"Verrrry carefully!"

Laughter bubbled out of him, and he swerved to a stop in the emergency parking lane. "Darling Kate," he said, taking her in his arms. "How do you always know the right thing to say when I'm acting like a fool?"

"Woman's intuition, I suppose . . . or love."

"I love you," he whispered, holding her gently and burying his face in her hair. They clung to each other like grateful survivors of some dread disaster, safe now in each other's arms.

Slowly, almost imperceptibly, she became aware of a sharp tapping sound. Something in her mind a long way off suggested: woodpecker? No, that wasn't it. It was more like something tapping on the windshield. She drew back from Giulio and looked over his shoulder.

A state trooper put his head in through Giulio's open window. His shoulders were as wide as the door. Kate could see herself and Giulio reflected in his mirrored sunglasses.

"This ain't no lovers' lane, buddy." The policeman's voice had the timbre of loose gravel.

"I know that, Officer—" Giulio began.

"I'm going to have to give you a citation for parking in the emergency lane."

"It's all my fault, Sergeant—Frinzi," said Kate, squinting at the nameplate pinned above his pocket. "I, uh, I just told my husband—Mr. Bond here—that we're going to have a baby, and I guess we got carried away." She could feel the blush as she said it rising right up to the roots of her hair. Fighting to keep a straight face, she glanced at Giulio. He looked pole-axed.

"Well!" said Sergeant Frinzi. Scrunching himself together and heaving his mighty shoulders through the window, he lunged for Kate's hand. "Congratulations, little lady!"

Kate winced as his belt buckle, a flight of mallards in antiqued brass, scraped against the car door, and she wondered uncharitably if the rental agency would deduct more or less than the cost of a ticket.

Frinzi wriggled himself back out through the window, pumping Giulio's hand as he went. "You two be careful now," he said with a smile as wide as a speeding ticket. "And have a nice day!"

Giulio turned to her, and his eyes were huge. "Kate, you're not—"

"Of course not, darling."

He let out a breath so long she thought he must have been holding it all this time. She couldn't tell if it was a sigh of relief or disappointment. He was quiet for several moments. Then, pulling back into the stream of traffic, he asked "Whatever possessed you to say that?"

"I didn't want you to get a ticket. It just popped into my head."

"I see," he murmured.

She snuggled next to him, pressing her cheek against his shoulder. "Have you switched aftershaves? You smell like bacon."

"I knew you'd like it," he said, his tone light again. "It's called *Essence de Lunch*."

"It's delicious," she said and sighed, sniffing his sweater. "Is that what's in the basket on the backseat?"

He nodded.

"I should have warned you—travel makes me ravenous. The minute I get in a car and drive five miles out of town, I'm starving." She lunged for the basket and settled it at her feet. "I'm convinced it has something to do with my nomadic Norwegian ancestors tramping across trackless miles of frozen tundra in search of reindeer."

"It's only egg salad and bacon sandwiches, and coffee."

"*Only,* the man says." She bit happily into a sandwich and passed one to Giulio.

"Do you remember," he said, "that first day when we had lunch?"

"I remember every mouthful."

"What I remember is how you tucked into your second helping of dal."

"Hmm. It was delicious."

"You had a tiny spot of sauce on your chin, and it nearly drove me crazy. I wanted to lean over and lick it off."

"You didn't."

"Oh, yes, I did. Then, when you came back to my office, all I could think about was how succulent your mouth looked."

"Darling, I think you're sex crazed."

"And the more you ranted about your independence, the more I wanted you."

"Do you mean you didn't even listen?"

"Oh, I listened. I listened and I said to myself, Giulio, that's the woman for you. She has *temperamento,* she's beautiful, and she eats like an Italian."

"I never guessed a thing. I thought you were being a very hard bargainer."

"Is that all? Didn't you feel the waves of animal magnetism I was sending out? This is where the gravy was." He ducked his head and licked the tip of her chin.

"Keep your eyes on the road, darling." Kate kissed a

crumb from the corner of his mouth and settled herself comfortably against his shoulder.

They drove in easy silence for some time before they finally turned off Pine Lane onto a rough track that wound through an unmown meadow that was pungent with wild thyme and bright with wild mustard and daisies.

"What's this like when it rains?" Giulio said with a grunt, maneuvering the front wheels out of a rut.

"It's a muddy mess. Dell and Hodge said I should order a load of crushed bluestone for it."

"Who are Dell and Hodge?"

"The friends I'm buying the house from. They live on the other side of the woods."

They carried the hampers inside. "As you can see," said Kate, "it's a very small house."

The ground floor was only two rooms, plus a stairway to the two bedrooms above. The cramped old parlor was barely big enough for a sagging couch in front of the fireplace, two equally sagging chairs, reading lamps with yellowed parchment shades, and an old table with a single straight-back chair.

"The kitchen's not bad," he said. It was large and airy, with an old pine table generous enough to seat eight. Pine cupboards and windows filled the three outside walls. Dell and Hodge had added plumbing, a shower, and a cast-off stove and refrigerator.

Giulio poked into every corner and cupboard, knocked on the walls, and thumped the beams. "It's a sound old house, but it's going to take a lot of work to fix it up," he said.

"Don't I know it! My next project's stripping the floors. There's wide-board pine under all that terrible brown paint."

"Is there anything below this floor?"

"An old root cellar."

"You know, that could make a good wine cellar if it's properly ventilated."

"Really?"

"And it would be easy for a contractor to open up the north side of the house and add a dining room downstairs here, and more bedrooms upstairs," he rushed on.

"But I *like* eating in the kitchen, and I don't *need* more bedrooms. So slow down, Bond." She caught his eye and saw the chagrin spread over his face.

"You're right, of course, Marple. I do tend to get pushy sometimes. You'll have to help me control that."

"Oh, I will, Bond. I will." She laughed and took his hand. "Come on outside and I'll show you my stream. Presumably you won't try to rearrange that part of my life," she teased.

A narrow path led through the fragrant meadow and into the woods. Giulio looked around at the birches and black spruce, maples, and oaks. "That should be culled out," he said, pointing to a blighted elm. Then he quickly looked at her in dismay.

Again she laughed, conceding, "It's okay this time. You're right about the tree."

Hand in hand they walked along through rushes and ferns, marsh marigold and wild parsley that lined the banks of a brook that rippled over small stones and swirled in eddies.

"Do you hear it?" said Kate.

He cocked his head and listened, a puzzled look on his face.

"It's my waterfall. It's only two feet high, but it's a real waterfall." They ducked under an overhanging willow and came upon a clear pool that was no more than eight feet across.

His voice was skeptical. "Is that where your trout hide? In that little thing?"

"They're not sharks," she defended, laughing and pulling him down to sit beside her on the bank. She lay on her back, looking up through a bower of wild lilacs at the sheltering branches high above. "Isn't this a heavenly place?" she said with a sigh.

Giulio rolled over onto his stomach and began examining the grass and moss with such infinite care he might have been searching for diamonds, so meticulously did his fingers part the leaves. He cleared his throat. "How old does a kid have to be to learn to fish like you do?"

"Fly fish? A girl might learn at eleven—I did—but boys usually aren't coordinated enough until about thirteen."

"That old?"

It was so still she could hear his breathing.

"Kate, do you remember that night before the theater party, when I said it didn't matter if you wouldn't live with me? I was lying to myself—it does matter. It matters more than anything in my life. I need you, Kate." His eyes were not pleading but proud. "I think I love you more than my life."

"Darling, I may still be a little frightened by the idea, but I'd move in tomorrow if I could get movers on a Sunday."

"Oh, Kate!" he shouted, smothering her in a bear hug. "It's going to be wonderful, you'll see. And you'll never have to eat another tuna casserole as long as you live. Of course, if you're really crazy for tuna I'll make you vitello tonnato or—Kate?"

"Hmm?"

"Are you frightened of me? Of my trying to subjugate you?"

"Not anymore. It may sound strange, but in opposing you I've somehow found the strength to honestly love you—and to stop being afraid of losing myself, my strength. It's mine to exercise or give, and the more freely I give it, the stronger I become."

"I promise you you'll always be free," he said, teasing the corners of her mouth with tiny kisses. "Even if I didn't want you to be, you wouldn't let me get away with anything else. You're stronger than you know. You always have been—you just needed to find out."

"So I've been told," she murmured, "by a certain art director, who called me tenacious and stubborn and—"

His lips cut off her diatribe, brushing hers as tenderly as they had the very first time, and she thrilled at the passion they promised. The days of emptiness and nights of longing were no more than a distant memory of pain that made the moment sweeter, her pleasure more exquisite, her need for him nearly unbearable. She lost all sense of place, all awareness of time. He pressed her yielding body into his, and she could feel him hard against her as she opened her mouth to him, their tongues like darting flames, kindling deeper fires.

He slipped his hands beneath her blouse to cup her breasts. "You have nothing on under this," he whispered with obvious delight.

"Neither do you," she said, sliding her hands beneath his shirt and flattening her palms against his bare back.

"Have you ever made love in the woods?" He unbuttoned her blouse, pushing it off her shoulders and kissing each of her breasts in turn.

"Never. I feel like a wood nymph."

Breaking off a clump of lilacs, he lightly stroked her body with the pale blossoms—ten thousand whispering kisses caressed her.

"You look like a wood nymph," he said, stripping the tiny flowers from their branches to let them cascade onto her breasts. *"Bella come un'aurora.* As beautiful as the dawn." He kissed the flowers away, delicately teasing her nipples with his teeth.

With tantalizing slowness, he drew off her remaining clothes, stroking them away. His kisses followed his hands in a sensuous game of tag, setting all her nerves afire. She pressed her hands over his shoulders and down his smooth, muscled back until she could grip his buttocks, hard and round as melons. He moaned deep in his chest and straightened enough to struggle out of his clothes. Then she drew him to her, arching her hips to meet the thrust of his. His mouth found hers again, and they became a single being—one in love, one in desire.

He called her name over and over, softly, rhythmically, matching his thrusting desire, until at the peak of his passion a hoarse, triumphant shout burst from his throat. Kate heard the startled birds skittering in the branches high above them and his cry, "I love you . . . love you . . . you . . . you . . . you . . ." echoing through the woods. Then she heard the little waterfall chuckling, and the birds returned.

"I love you," she whispered. "We'll never lose each other again."

The air was soft, the birds of early twilight had begun to call, and the sun had not quite touched the hills. Kate wanted this moment to go on forever, so rich was it with love, with promise of the future stretching before them. Night hawks swooped through the still air, and the evening star hung sharp and brilliant in the darkening sky.

He kissed her deeply, and she shuddered in a spasm of desire.

"Are you cold?" he asked. "Shall we go back?"

"No, it's warm, darling. Don't move. I want to stay like this forever. I feel—enchanted." She could not say where her love ended and his began. She could not tell where his body ended and hers began. We'll rise up into the sky, she thought. We'll burst into a thousand glinting fragments around the evening star and become a constellation to mark the sky for lovers.

"Tell me," he whispered. "What do you hear?"

Kate listened. She could hear the calls of early night birds, the thrum of insects, the first crickets measuring the end of day. "I hear the twilight coming," she said at last.

"Do you know what's missing?" he said. "What you don't hear?"

"Hmm?"

"The laughter of children . . . Dearest Kate, will you marry me?"

"Yes, darling, yes."

It grew dim in their lilac chamber, the heavy flowers all around them moving gently in the sun's last rays.

"We begin from today," she said. Their love was a grace in the scented air around them; the sunlight a drowsy, winking syrup lumpy with bees.

"From this moment," he said, and before she could answer, his mouth covered hers and he took her in a shower of blossoms.

_____ 06864-0 **A PROMISE TO CHERISH** #100 LaVyrle Spencer
_____ 06866-7 **BELOVED STRANGER** #102 Michelle Roland
_____ 06867-5 **ENTHRALLED** #103 Ann Cristy
_____ 06869-1 **DEFIANT MISTRESS** #105 Anne Devon
_____ 06870-5 **RELENTLESS DESIRE** #106 Sandra Brown
_____ 06871-3 **SCENES FROM THE HEART** #107 Marie Charles
_____ 06872-1 **SPRING FEVER** #108 Simone Hadary
_____ 06873-X **IN THE ARMS OF A STRANGER** #109 Deborah Joyce
_____ 06874-8 **TAKEN BY STORM** #110 Kay Robbins
_____ 06899-3 **THE ARDENT PROTECTOR** #111 Amanda Kent
_____ 07200-1 **A LASTING TREASURE** #112 Cally Hughes $1.95
_____ 07203-6 **COME WINTER'S END** #115 Claire Evans $1.95
_____ 07212-5 **SONG FOR A LIFETIME** #124 Mary Haskell $1.95
_____ 07213-3 **HIDDEN DREAMS** #125 Johanna Phillips $1.95
_____ 07214-1 **LONGING UNVEILED** #126 Meredith Kingston $1.95
_____ 07215-X **JADE TIDE** #127 Jena Hunt $1.95
_____ 07216-8 **THE MARRYING KIND** #128 Jocelyn Day $1.95
_____ 07217-6 **CONQUERING EMBRACE** #129 Ariel Tierney $1.95
_____ 07218-4 **ELUSIVE DAWN** #130 Kay Robbins $1.95
_____ 07219-2 **ON WINGS OF PASSION** #131 Beth Brookes $1.95
_____ 07220-6 **WITH NO REGRETS** #132 Nuria Wood $1.95
_____ 07221-4 **CHERISHED MOMENTS** #133 Sarah Ashley $1.95
_____ 07222-2 **PARISIAN NIGHTS** #134 Susanna Collins $1.95
_____ 07233-0 **GOLDEN ILLUSIONS** #135 Sarah Crewe $1.95
_____ 07224-9 **ENTWINED DESTINIES** #136 Rachel Wayne $1.95
_____ 07225-7 **TEMPTATION'S KISS** #137 Sandra Brown $1.95
_____ 07226-5 **SOUTHERN PLEASURES** #138 Daisy Logan $1.95
_____ 07227-3 **FORBIDDEN MELODY** #139 Nicola Andrews $1.95
_____ 07228-1 **INNOCENT SEDUCTION** #140 Cally Hughes $1.95
_____ 07229-X **SEASON OF DESIRE** #141 Jan Mathews $1.95
_____ 07230-3 **HEARTS DIVIDED** #142 Francine Rivers $1.95
_____ 07231-1 **A SPLENDID OBSESSION** #143 Francesca Sinclaire $1.95
_____ 07232-X **REACH FOR TOMORROW** #144 Mary Haskell $1.95
_____ 07233-8 **CLAIMED BY RAPTURE** #145 Marie Charles $1.95
_____ 07234-6 **A TASTE FOR LOVING** #146 Frances Davies $1.95
_____ 07235-4 **PROUD POSSESSION** #147 Jena Hunt $1.95

All of the above titles are $1.75 per copy except where noted

---

Available at your local bookstore or return this form to:

 SECOND CHANCE AT LOVE
Book Mailing Service
P.O. Box 690, Rockville Centre, NY 11571

Please send me the titles checked above. I enclose _____
**Include $1.00 for postage and handling if one book is ordered; 50¢ per book for
two or more. California, Illinois, New York and Tennessee residents please add
sales tax.**

NAME _____

ADDRESS _____

CITY _____ STATE/ZIP _____
(allow six weeks for delivery)

SK-41b